WAKE UP AND SPELL THE COFFEE

ENCHANTED ENCLAVE MYSTERY #1

SAMANTHA SILVER

CHAPTER 1

I woke up on the morning of my first day at my first ever job anxious and ready to go. I had no idea what a nightmare it was going to turn out to be, or that it was going to result in my life being completely turned upside-down.

I'd gone through a lot of life changes, recently. I graduated from college three months ago, and the day after he watched me cross that stage, my father died of a heart attack. Dad had raised me by himself after my mother died when I was a baby, and his death hit me hard.

A part of me didn't want life to keep going. A part of me wanted to continue hiding under the blankets, crying, and wishing things were different every day until it was finally my turn to go. But I knew Dad wouldn't have wanted me to live that way. He would have wanted me to go out and make something of myself, to live my dreams.

That was how I had ended up here, working as a receptionist at a small physiotherapy office in a local mall. It certainly wasn't me living my dreams. It wasn't even a job I wanted, but it was a job, and frankly that was fine with me for now. I wasn't sure I could mentally handle anything more complex than answering the phones, making appointments and handling payments for people, so when I was offered the position I decided to take it.

I arrived ten minutes early that morning, wearing my best pair of black slacks and a dark purple blouse. Despite the fact that I had just turned twenty-three years old, I had never actually had a job before.

Dad had always insisted that he pay for my entire education and living costs – it helped that I was able to live at home while going to college – so that I could focus on my studies. I was very aware of just how lucky I was to have a father both willing and able to do such a thing for me, but as a result, while all my peers had experience working everywhere from McDonald's to the local library, I had an extra layer of nerves to deal with. There was no denying it: I had lived a sheltered, coddled life, and I was now nervous going out into the real world for the first time.

I knocked on the locked front door, and a moment later a perky woman in her late twenties with way black hair and friendly round eyes opened it up for me.

"Hi, you must be Elizabeth," she said, holding out a hand. "I'm Emma."

"Call me Eliza, please," I replied, shaking her hand. "It's nice to meet you."

"You too," she said, motioning for me to enter. I did as she requested and looked around. Oasis Physiotherapy looked very clinical, with white-painted walls and a shelf against the wall on the left displaying various items for sale – kinesiology tape, ankle wraps, knee braces, slings, that sort of thing. The wall to the right featured various awards the place had won, as well as framed photos of athletes, signed along with messages of thanks for ensuring the athlete in question was able to return to their sport of choice after an injury.

Straight ahead was a long reception desk, with a couple of chairs behind it.

"So most of your job here is going to be to answer the phone," Emma told me as she motioned for me to follow her behind the desk. "Most of the calls are either to make appointments, or asking about the services we offer. Our job also involves setting up the physiotherapy rooms for the next clients, but I figure it's best to let you master the stuff behind the desk before I show you that part."

"Thanks," I said gratefully, sitting down in one of the chairs and looking at the computers. "So this is the appointment system?"

"That's right; let me give you a quick crash course on how it works."

Twenty minutes later I was feeling somewhat confident in my ability to schedule an appointment, but when the machine rang and Emma motioned for me to pick up, I still froze for a second.

"Go on," she said kindly. "You've got this."

My hand moved toward the phone as if someone else was controlling my body. The next thing I knew the handset was pressed against my ear.

"Hell-hello?" I said slowly, my mouth feeling like it was full of cotton balls. At the last second I realized that was absolutely not the greeting Emma had taught me, and I added it on quickly. "Thank you for calling Oasis Physiotherapy, how can I help you this morning?"

Emma gave me a thumbs up as she sat down in the other chair, and my confidence began to grow from there. I had successfully uttered a single sentence without messing it up too badly. When, a couple of minutes later, I had successfully made an appointment for the woman on the other end of the line, I felt a strong sense of accomplishment. Maybe I wasn't going to be the worst person ever at this whole 'having a job' thing after all.

The rest of the morning passed by uneventfully as I got increasingly comfortable with my job, and eventually my heart even stopped skipping a beat every time the phone rang.

"You're a quick learner," Emma told me approvingly after a couple of hours. "Good job."

It was right after I came back from my break, at around one in the afternoon, that everything went nuts.

A woman had come in, along with her son who looked to be about six years old. He was carrying one of those individual-sized cartons of cereal, and dropped it on the floor in front of the reception desk. As the cereal spilled out on the floor, the boy burst into tears, his mother immediately picking him up and consoling him. I jumped up, looking over at Emma.

"Where's the broom?" I asked instinctively, and she pointed at the storage cupboard next to me. I opened it and grabbed the plain wooden broom and dustpan. I had to fight back tears at the sight. One of Dad's weird quirks was his hatred for brooms. He had never allowed them in the house, insisting that vacuum cleaners, a mop and a Swiffer were all we needed. I had never understood why he was so opposed to brooms being available, and pulling this one out of the closet now made me think of him, and how much my life was changing now that he was gone.

But no, I couldn't dwell on that fact. I blinked back the tears and tried not to think about my dad. I had to keep it together, or my new coworkers would be convinced I was a crazy person and I'd be let go before I knew it.

Instead, I focused on cleaning up the spilled Raisin Bran on the ground.

"It's ok, buddy," I said to the little boy, who gazed up at me with big, black eyes lined with red. Obviously, losing his cereal treat was the worst thing to have ever happened to him in his short life. I flashed him the kindest smile I could, and he sniffled once before trying to smile at me in return. It appeared the worst of it was over.

The broom felt a little bit strange in my hand, almost like it was buzzing with energy. But that was ridiculous; it was a broom. Brooms didn't have energy. I knelt down to place the duster on the floor, and as soon as I did, the broom began to move on its own.

"What the-?" I called out in surprise as the next thing I knew the broom was pulling me along the floor.

"Eliza!" I heard Emma shout from the counter, but it was too hate. I was being dragged toward the doorway and out into the main entrance to the mall. The broom was picking up speed with every passing foot, and I had no idea what to do.

What on earth was going on? A part of me wanted to let go, but I was somehow frozen. My hands wouldn't obey my brain as I began zipping through the mall attached to a broom that was flying around as if by magic. A squeal of fear escaped my lips as the broom darted around surprised shoppers who appeared as barely more than blurs in front of my eyes. Startled passersby stopped to watch as the broom dragged me along, my feet glancing along the floor as it floated through the expansive hallway toward the escalators.

Fear rose in my throat as I was dragged closer toward it. Was I going to crash right into it? I had to let go. And yet, my hands wouldn't let go of the broom. Instead, I squeezed my eyes shut and waited for the inevitable thud which never came. When I finally dared to open them once more, I let out another yelp.

The broom had gone straight ahead instead of taking the escalator up or down, and I was now hanging about twenty feet in the air, above the food court. Shocked diners stood and pointed as the broom began flying in a circle in the atrium above the dining area, with me now clinging desperately onto it for dear life. If I let go now, it was going to be a long fall onto the ground below.

Rather than imagining myself pitching to the ground and dying a gruesome death surrounded by old trays and KFC wrappers, I swung my legs upwards and wrapped them around the broom for extra security. The broom then did a quick barrel roll before spinning around on itself and coming to a stop, floating in the air, and I found myself sitting on top of the broom, clutching onto it for dear life like the world's most terrified and incompetent witch.

Multiple security guards wandered underneath me, looking upwards, obviously at a loss of what to do. "Ma'am, we're going to need you to come down from there," one of them called up toward me.

"I can't," I shouted back. "I don't know what's going on."

"Look, I don't know what kind of trick you think you're playing, but Halloween was months ago. Please come down from there."

"I'm telling you," I cried, panic rising in my voice. "I have no idea how. I don't know why this is happening. Help me."

"Alright, we're going to call the fire department, and they're going to come and get you. Hold tight."

Oh, I was definitely holding tight. My knuckles were white and my ankles were locked together so tightly the firefighters would need the Jaws of Life to get them separated. Why couldn't I have let go of the broom earlier? I never would have found myself in this situation.

I began to cry as the onlookers gawked at me and dropped my head down out of shame. To my immense surprise, the broom began moving again, and I shrieked as the shame was replaced with a new wave of fear as I held on for dear life. The broom swept downwards, plummeting toward one of the dining tables. I squeezed my eyes shut, not wanting to see what was about to happen, but at the last second the broom leveled out, sweeping straight through the table and sending glasses of pop, French fries and burger wrappers flying everywhere. The family sitting at the table let out a shout as they did their best to escape the carnage, while my brown hair now dripped with Coke, and I was fairly sure there were a few fries stuck in it as well.

The broom took a left and headed down the main hallway. Shoppers plastered themselves against the wall as I zoomed past, before finally reaching the elaborate, two-story high fountain in the center atrium of the mall. The broom zoomed straight underneath the thick current of water, soaking me to the bone, and the shock of the cold water caused me to let go of the broom.

I fell straight into the fountain, the cold water bringing me to a quick stop, but pain still seared through one of my arms as I hit the edge. I inhaled sharply, sending fountain water down my throat, and spluttered it all back up, arms and legs flailing around like a baby giraffe on its back. When I finally regained control of my body I was sitting on the bottom of the fountain in water that almost reached up to my shoulders. My wrist hurt like crazy, there were French fries in my hair, and dozens of people gawked while mall security rushed toward me.

The broom that had caused this whole ruckus floated in the fountain next to me like nothing had happened.

And yet, it had happened.

What on earth was going on?

CHAPTER 2

"Excuse me miss, you're going to have to come with us," one of the security guards said to me. I looked him up and down. He was older, probably in his fifties, with a beer belly that was more keg than pint glass. His thumbs were pressed into his belt loops, and he stuck out his stomach like he thought it made him look more intimidating.

The other security guard was a scrawny-looking man who looked to be about my age and obviously couldn't have cared less about being there. He looked around casually.

"I'm sorry," I said. "I don't know what happened."

"Yeah, yeah," the first guard replied. "That's what they all say. And yet here you've caused all this mischief, and ruined one family's lunch. Mall management will be pressing mischief charges, so come along now. Steven, grab that broom, as well. It's evidence. I'm sure we'll find a motor or something inside."

The other security guard made his way to the fountain and reached toward the broom, obviously trying to grab it without getting his shoes wet. My mind swam as I considered what the security guard had just told me. Charges being filed? I was going to be *arrested*? But I had no idea what had even happened. None of this was my fault. I looked over at the broom as Steven grabbed it, but nothing happened. It was just a normal, plain old run-of-the-mill wooden broom.

This could *not* be happening to me. It was my first day at my new job, and now I was going to be arrested? There had to be a mistake. I would go with the security guards, I would explain to them what had happened, apologize to the family, and then everything would be fine.

Except I didn't know what had happened. All I knew was that as soon as I had grabbed the broom it had dragged me along for the worst ride of my life.

"Come on, let's get going," the first security guard muttered. "What are you, slow or something?"

I followed after the security guards, completely humiliated as shoppers gawked while I walked past, their eyes boring into me. My water-logged shoes squished with every step, and my clothes dripped onto the tiles. The only good thing about the water was that it masked my tears of complete and total humiliation. Thankfully, I hadn't wet my pants. That would be the only thing that could make this embarrassment any more complete.

I had considered running away, trying to make a mad dash for the door and hoping that no one would ever find out who I was, but of course, Oasis Physiotherapy had all of my personal information. Mall security would be able to find me easily, and if I fled now, even if I managed to get away, it was only a matter of time before I'd have the police knocking at my door.

Going with the security guards and begging for forgiveness and mercy seemed like the best way to go.

"Come on, keep up," the first guard scolded as I trudged along after them. One of the bystanders caught my eye; I looked up to see a short woman who looked to be in her fifties. Her formerly brown hair was now liberally speckled with grey, and despite her short stature she had a way about her. She stood out in the room, and her brown eyes twinkled at me. The corners of her lips seemed to flicker up into a bit of a smile, but I couldn't tell if she was mocking me or supporting me.

I made my way past her and followed the two security guards into their office. It was small, with two chairs behind a double-length desk, and a third chair sitting against the wall. On the desk sat a box of a dozen donuts; eleven of them were left.

"Great, do you have to spill water all over the floor? Steve, go get a mop, this is ridiculous." I wanted to sit down, but I had a feeling the security guard wouldn't like me getting the thin cloth layer on the chair against the wall wet. "So, what kind of stupid prank did you think this was?" he asked me, plunking himself down in one of the chairs behind the desk. The chair wheezed, obviously struggling under the man's weight.

"I swear," I pleaded. "I have absolutely no idea what happened. I work at Oasis Physiotherapy. Today was my first day. I just grabbed the broom to clean up a mess and the next thing I knew I was flying through the mall. I don't know what happened. Please, you have to believe me. I'm so sorry for all of this. I don't know what happened, I really don't."

The man sighed, then glanced up at me without moving his head. "Seriously, lady. I really don't want to deal with this today. The cops are a phone call away. Just tell me what happened, for real, and maybe we can make a deal."

"A deal?" I asked. I so desperately did not want to get arrested for this. I was only twenty-three years old. I had my whole life in front of me. A deal sounded absolutely amazing.

"Yes, I think we can organize something. How about you pay for the damage you've caused here today, and we can just let the whole thing slide under the table. How does that sound?"

"Great," I said, practically shouting from excitement.

"Calm down, calm down. Geez. Look, I think we can all agree you cost this mall a lot of money. Why don't we call it an even thousand? You give me that in cash, right now, and you can walk out of here."

The excitement I'd felt a moment ago drained from my body. A thousand dollars? I didn't have that kind of money. All of the estate stuff with my dad hadn't been settled yet – although immediately after he passed I had been given a few thousand dollars by his lawyer as an advance for living expenses - and since I'd only graduated a few months ago and hadn't started working yet I was running pretty low on funds. I had a few hundred bucks to my name, but I certainly didn't have a thousand.

"A thousand? But all I did was ruin that one family's lunch," I argued.

"Well, there was that, but you also caused emotional damage to many people," the man replied. "Besides, I'm not here to argue with you. Either hand over the cash, or I can call the cops."

I had a sneaking suspicion the cash was going to go straight into the security guard's pocket.

"I don't have that kind of money," I said in a small voice. "I can't pay you that much."

The man sighed. "Seriously? Look, I'm giving you an out here. Just pay me the thousand bucks and I don't have to do the paperwork involved with handing you over to the cops."

I shrugged. "I can't give you what I don't have."

"Ask your family, or something. I'll even drop it to seven-fifty. Look, this works out better for both of us.

You get to keep a clean record, and I don't have to spend my afternoon filling out forms I don't want to fill out."

Family. My eyes welled with tears. There was no one else. Only Dad and me. And now Dad was gone, and I didn't know what to do. This was my first attempt at living life on my own, living my life without him, and I had already screwed it up so insanely badly there was a good chance I was going to jail.

Tears sprang to my eyes and started flowing.

"Oh, great. Now you're crying. Look, it doesn't have to be this bad, ok? I'm trying to help you, even though you're dripping all over the floor. Come on. I really don't want to have to deal with this today."

I wiped at the tears forming in my eyes, when all of a sudden the donuts in the box in front of the security guard began floating in the air.

"What on earth?" he said, his attention moving from me to the baked goods. "Are you doing this? What is wrong with you? How is this happening?"

I could only shake my head, at a complete loss for words. I had no idea what was going on. Why were the donuts flying? Was this just the worst dream ever, and I was going to wake up in my bed drenched in sweat in a few minutes? It certainly *felt* real.

Suddenly, the donuts began zooming around the room, like a bunch of trapped birds doing their best to escape. I ducked out of the way at the last second, narrowly avoiding being hit fair in the face by a Boston

Crème which splattered against the wall behind me a second later, yellow cream squirting out of the donut like it had just been murdered.

I dropped to the floor to minimize my odds of getting hit by any more baked projectiles while the security guard jumped around, trying to grab the donuts out of midair. An apple fritter was teasing him, darting around his head in circles, always avoiding the guard's chubby hands as he grabbed at it repeatedly.

The other guard, Steve, had straight-up passed out at the sight of the flying donuts and was now lying in a crumpled heap on the floor.

A chocolate glazed suddenly veered off-course and landed straight in the first guard's face, causing him to shout out and lose his balance. He fell backwards, hitting the ground with a loud thud, and as soon as he did the donuts all dive-bombed him, but before I had a chance to see what kind of state the security guard was in, the door opened behind me.

This could not be good. The last thing I wanted to explain to anybody was why the guard was currently lying on the ground, surrounded by the remains of suicidal donuts.

But the person standing in the doorway was the woman from earlier, with the greying hair. She held a stick in her hand, about a foot long, covered in blue glitter, and she didn't seem the least bit perturbed about the scene she'd come across. In fact, when one final vanilla dipped donut appeared out of nowhere and started zooming around, a small whistling sound coming from the hole in the center of it, she simply waved the stick at the donut and it fell to the ground.

I gaped at her. "Is… what…" I had so many questions, but at the same time, I didn't even know what those questions *were*.

"Did you just stop that donut with your stick? How come the donuts were flying? Did you do that? What are you doing here? What happened with the broom?"

The witch gave me a kindly smile. "Why don't we get out of here, and I'll answer your questions. I'm sure you have a lot of them. But first, let me take care of this." She pointed her wand right at me, and all of a sudden I went from soaking wet with fries in my hair to looking like the professional I had been just a couple of hours earlier.

I gasped as I looked at my clothes. "How on earth?" I asked. "What are you doing? What *are* you?"

"My name is Lucy Marcet, and I belong to the coven of Saturn. I'm a witch, and your aunt. It's nice to see you again, Eliza."

CHAPTER 3

Nope. None of this was happening. None of this was real. The woman had just told me she was my aunt, and a witch? That wasn't possible. I didn't have an aunt. My parents had both been only children. Oh, and there was that whole thing about *witches not being real*.

Maybe I was on a really, *really* bad trip. I didn't do drugs, but what if some had been added to the sandwich I had for lunch by accident? That was a thing that could happen, right?

"Come on," Lucy said to me, motioning for me to follow her. "This big oaf is going to wake up any minute now."

She had a point there, and I followed the crazy woman as we made our way back into the mall.

"Where would you like to go to chat?" she asked me kindly.

"Literally anywhere that's not here," I replied. I had to get out of this mall. I kept looking at my clothes. Maybe they hadn't been wet in the first place. Maybe I was imagining the whole thing. That could have happened, right? Because the idea that Lucy had used magic to dry them was insane. Completely insane. That wasn't possible.

I followed her out of the mall, and into a nearby coffee shop. She went to the counter to order, and I took a closer look at her. Lucy was dressed in jeans and a light sweater; probably a little bit overdressed for the weather here in San Francisco in late February, but not so insane that it threw up a red flag. She was a shade under five feet tall, but carried herself with the confidence of someone who knew exactly who she was. Nothing about her screamed 'insane', so I figured it was probably safe to have coffee with her. At least we were in a public location. Besides, it was possible *I* was the crazy one in this situation. After all, I had no idea what had happened over the last hour or so. Had I gone insane? Was I hallucinating? Maybe I had pushed myself too hard to get back into the real world after Dad died.

Lucy came back just then with a couple of lattes. She placed one in front of me and I tried to be subtle as I sniffed it carefully for traces of any foreign smells. I took a sip, but it tasted normal.

"Now, I'm sure you have questions," Lucy said softly. "Do you want me to tell you what's happened?"

I nodded. "Yes, please. Am I insane? Have I been drugged? What's going on?"

"You're not insane and you haven't been drugged. Frankly, I enjoyed the show – what I saw of it, anyway. You're a witch, Eliza, and I'm your aunt. Your mother was my sister."

"No," I said, shaking my head. "My mom didn't have any sisters."

"She did," Lucy replied. "In fact, she had two sisters, and a brother."

"Magic isn't real."

"Magic is real," Lucy replied. "You were born into a family of witches. Why do you think the broom acted the way it did when you touched it?"

"I don't know," I had to admit. "I have no idea what happened."

"Brooms are designed to move when witches touch them. If you had been raised as a witch, you would have learned how to control them and fly them by now."

"But that doesn't make sense. Magic just is not real."

Lucy smiled at me and pulled out that stick again. "Watch this."

She looked around and pointed the wand at her coffee cup, which immediately turned into a bat, which flapped its wings and started streaking around the coffee shop.

Lucy didn't seem the least bit bothered about the chaos she'd just caused as the bat flapped around the shop. Half the customers cowered under the tables while an enterprising barista tried – and failed – to trap it in a small box to let it outside.

"Where did that thing come from?" someone asked.

"Someone get that thing out of here?"

"What if it flies into my coffee?"

"This is unhygienic!"

"That coffee was decidedly sub-par anyway," Lucy said with a shrug. "Only the undead would want to drink it."

I gaped at her. "How did you do that?"

"I told you, magic. Your mother was a witch, and you are too."

"What do you know about my mother?" I asked, my eyes narrowing. I was absolutely not going to take this woman at face value, especially when I wasn't sure what I could trust and what I couldn't. This entire day was so insane I wasn't going to trust anything I didn't have to.

"Your mother's name was Patricia, maiden name Marcet. She met your father at Enchanted Enclave, an island where they both grew up. Your mother died in a car accident when you were six months old, and your father moved you to San Francisco immediately after that."

My throat was dry. Everything she had said matched what my father had told me. Although I had never heard of Enchanted Enclave. He told me we had lived in Seattle.

"He never told me she had family," I said, and Lucy nodded.

"Your father never truly came to grips with the fact that your mother was a witch," Lucy replied. "He hated it when she used it around him, and when she died, he moved to get you away from the family influence. He wanted you to grow up like the human he was, and never intended for you to find out about your powers."

Suddenly, Dad's dislike of brooms made sense. A lot of things clicked, actually. Like when I started reading Harry Potter books when I was in fourth grade. Dad had told me it was fine, but I had noticed the way his lips pressed together when he saw me with those books, and how he would occasionally mutter curses at the TV when he saw Sabrina the Teenage Witch reruns show up on the guide.

"So mom had family?" I asked quietly.

"That's right," Lucy said. "There's me, and your other aunt Debbie. She's not nearly as much fun as I am, though. Then there's your Uncle Robert. He can be a real stick in the mud, too. None of them would find the situation with the bat hilarious at all."

The coffee-cup-turned-bat had at some point been released outside, and normalcy was returning to the coffee shop about as quickly as it seemed to be escaping from my life.

Could this possibly be real, or was I about to wake up from the world's weirdest dream?

"You also have two cousins," Lucy continued.

"Kaillie and Leanne. Kaillie spends all her time worrying about the stupid curse, and Leanne has no magical powers at all since Robert is her father, but they're alright all the same."

"Wait, a curse?" I asked, but Lucy waved a hand.

"You don't need to worry about that right now. Anyway, once you finish your coffee, I'll help you pack, and we can head back to Enchanted Enclave Island together."

"What?" I asked quietly. "No, I can't go with you."

Lucy tilted her head toward me. "Why not? You've just discovered you're a witch, and we're the only people in the world who can teach you how to use your powers. Why wouldn't you want to come with me?"

"What if I don't want to learn to use these powers?" I asked, my voice barely more than a whisper. "What if Dad had a good reason to stop me from knowing about them?" I couldn't help but feel that if I accepted this magic I was betraying his memory. He had done his absolute best to raise me all by himself, and he had obviously had a reason for stopping me from knowing these people. Would I be doing his memory a disservice by going with Lucy?

"Well, that's just ridiculous," she replied. "We're your family. Who do you have here?"

She had a point there. But my entire life had always been Dad and me. Us against the world, making it despite everything going against us. I could do things by myself. I could make it. Right?

I couldn't help but think about the niggling voice in the back of my head telling me it was easier with family. Dad had always been there for me, and now that he was gone, I was struggling. I couldn't deny that. I had managed to fail at my first day on the job. There was no point in going back to the mall. Best case scenario I was fired, worst case scenario the cops were sitting there waiting for me. What else did I have going for me in life? I had an English literature degree, a couple of followers on Instagram but no one I would really call a friend, and my dad's ashes in an urn on the fireplace. Even I had to admit that wasn't much of a life.

So why not give this 'family' thing a shot? What was the worst that could happen?

CHAPTER 4

"Alright," I finally said to Lucy. "I'll go with you. But I do have one more question: how did you find me?"

"I had a sneaking suspicion your father was going to sneak you away from Enchanted Enclave when your mother died," Lucy replied. "I set up a magical tracker on you, but it would only activate when you used magic. I honestly thought you would have accidentally triggered it earlier than now."

"Dad didn't let us have a broom around the house," I said with a shrug.

"He probably suspected," Lucy said. "Your father never trusted me. He always thought I would be a bad influence on his daughter."

"Are you?" I asked.

"Absolutely," Lucy replied. "As soon as the tracker

activated I used magic to get over here. I saw the last of your little adventure in the mall."

I shook my head, trying to get the memory of what had happened out of it. "That was so embarrassing."

"Oh I don't know, from where I was standing it was quite hilarious. You are lucky you didn't hurt yourself falling off that broom, though. It was a good thing the fountain was there to help break your fall."

"Yeah, a good thing," I muttered, rolling my wrist around. Most of the pain I had initially felt had disappeared, luckily.

"Now, I'm sure you have some stuff to bring with you, but we can organize that later," Lucy said. "Why don't you head on home, pack some of the essentials for now, and we'll take care of the rest another time. I'm sure you're anxious to meet the rest of your family."

I wasn't sure anxious was the right word. Apprehensive was maybe more accurate. Was I running into something I shouldn't be just because I had one bad day? I had never had a real family before. Just Dad. He was all the family I had ever needed. What if I hated all of these people? What if we didn't get along? What would I do then?

I supposed I could always move back here. Nothing was stopping me from doing that. I could go to Enchanted Enclave, meet these people I was related to and see how I felt afterwards.

"Sure," I said. "Let me just go pack a quick bag."

An hour later I was in the front doorway to my dad's house, a large duffel bag in front of me packed with the clothes and essentials I'd need for a couple of weeks. If I hated life at Enchanted Enclave I could always come back here. I kept telling myself that.

"How are we getting back there, anyway?" I asked Lucy. "Do you have a car or something?"

"I have something way better," she said with a wink, pulling out her wand. I balked at the sight.

"No, no way. You can't use magic to travel."

"Why not? That's how I got here so fast."

I took a deep breath, closed my eyes for a second, then opened them once more. "I'm not comfortable with this at all."

"Magic is a part of your life now, Eliza. You're going to have to get used to it." Then, she pointed her wand at me. *"Saturn, god of plenty, send this witch home, where she can meet Debbie."*

I didn't feel anything, but a split second later I was no longer standing in the entryway to my childhood home. Instead, I was in the kitchen of a large house, the smell of roast beef wafting toward my nostrils. The large, modern kitchen in front of me was part of a cabin-style home with high ceilings, adorned with exposed beams. Warm light flowed through the space, and standing in front of the stove with her back to me was a woman with curly brown hair, humming to herself.

I coughed lightly, trying to get her attention, and she turned a moment later. The instant her eyes landed on me her mouth dropped open and the spatula in her hand fell to the floor.

"It can't be," she whispered. "Eliza?"

"That's me," I offered with an awkward smile. A moment later Lucy appeared, holding my duffel bag in one hand and her wand in the other.

"Ah, Debbie. Good, you're home. Meet Eliza. I hope you made enough; she's staying for dinner, and for the rest of her life."

"Well, I'm not so sure about that just yet," I muttered, but it was too late. Debbie had already taken me into a big bear hug, and I had to say, after the day I'd had, it felt good. I let my body relax and sink into her warm, comfortable arms.

"Oh my dear, it is so good to see you after all these years," she muttered into my ear as she held me close. "I've missed you so much."

Ok, so even though I wasn't totally sold on this whole family thing, tears welled into my eyes at that. Maybe it was just leftover emotion from the day, but I quickly found myself crying into Debbie's shoulder as she held me close. "It's alright dear," she kept saying. "It's alright."

"So you were one of my mom's sisters?" I asked Debbie when I finally pulled away, and she nodded.

"That's right. Patricia was older than me by a year. Lucy's the oldest of us all; she's pushing sixty."

"Ah, but I'm the youngest at heart," the older witch replied.

"If we're going by maturity level, certainly," Debbie replied. "But come now; all Lucy told us before she left was that she sensed you use your powers. How did you come to find you were a witch?"

"I'd rather not say," I mumbled, expecting a bit of pushback.

"Well, that's quite alright then," Debbie replied, finally picking the spatula up off the floor and putting it in the sink. "I imagine you must have so many questions about your past. I assume your father never told you about your powers?"

"That's right," I replied, a little bit defensively.

"Well, he had his reasons, I'm sure. It was quite a shock for him when Patricia told him the truth, and he never quite got used to the idea of magic being real, I think."

I began to relax slightly; Debbie seemed to be the kindest, most understanding woman in the world.

"Now, you're going to need somewhere to stay. Luckily, we have some extra rooms. It won't take much to get a bed made up, let me take you upstairs for now. Your cousins live in a small house down the street, I'm sure they'll be happy to have you move in with them more permanently if you'd like. But for now you can stay with me, for as long as you need to get settled."

Debbie led me up a set of stairs to a gorgeous room with an attached bathroom. A bare king-sized mattress sat on a four-poster frame, and a moment later Debbie pulled out a wand of her own – a plain white one with a single black stripe down the side – and muttered a spell. I made out the words 'Saturn' and 'bedsheets' and a moment later a set of navy blue sheets flew out from the closet and attached themselves perfectly to the bed, followed closely by a couple of thick blankets.

"There," Debbie said, satisfied. "This is your room for as long as you need it."

"Thanks," I replied. "That spell could have come in handy a few times as a kid."

Debbie laughed. "It comes in handy as an adult, too. I'll teach you, of course. We're going to have to teach you everything, I suppose. You really had no idea you were a witch until today?"

I shook my head.

"Well, in that case, I'm sure you've got a lot to process and you probably want some alone time. Dinner will be ready in half an hour if you want to come down then. You're welcome earlier, of course, but if you'd rather get used to your new surroundings, that's fine as well."

"Thanks, I think I might have a shower," I said. I still wasn't entirely convinced that this wasn't the world's longest dream, and maybe jumping into the shower would bring me back to reality. Maybe this whole day had never happened.

"I'll be downstairs if you need anything," Debbie

said, closing the door behind me. I stepped into the shower, but didn't wake up. Maybe this was all real after all.

It was going to take some getting used to.

CHAPTER 5

Half an hour later I made my way back downstairs to find the crowd in the house had grown. There was Debbie, of course, and Lucy – I wondered if I shouldn't start calling them Aunt Debbie and Aunt Lucy – but they had been joined by a man who had the same eyes and nose as Aunt Debbie. His mouth was thinner, but turned up into a friendly smile. Next to him were a couple of women around my age, speaking to one another.

"Hi, you must be Eliza," the man said, striding toward me and holding out a hand, which I took. "I'm Robert, your uncle. You're more than welcome to just call me Bob, though."

"Hi, Bob," I said. His grip was firm and confident, and he smiled at me with a pride I didn't really feel I deserved.

"Let me introduce you to your two cousins. Girls,"

he called out, and the two women made their way over. "This is Leanne, my daughter," he said, motioning to the one on the right. She had the same mouth as Bob did, and the same reddish-blond hair. She grinned at me.

"Hi. It's nice to meet you. I was hoping I'd finally have another family member who can't use magic, but I guess that hasn't quite worked out for me."

"You're not a witch?" I asked, and Leanne shook her head.

"No, I drew the genetic short straw. Apparently, magical powers only descend through the maternal side of the family, and since my magical ancestor is my dad I don't get to play in the cool kids' sandbox."

"Oh come on, Leanne," the other girl laughed. "It's not that bad."

"Spoken like someone who would have had the ability to hex Mrs. Greyson if she caught you cheating on that test in eighth grade," Leanne replied.

The other girl gasped. "That was you who did that! I would never, ever cheat on a test."

"We all know that, Kaillie," Leanne grinned. "Anyway, you're being rude. Introduce yourself to your cousin."

"I'm so sorry," Kaillie said, obviously flustered. "I'm Kaillie. It's really nice to meet you. I'm Debbie's daughter, and unlike Leanne here, I'm also a witch, and I'm happy to teach you everything I can." She beamed at me from behind a heart-shaped face covered in freckles, and wavy brown hair like her mother's."

"Hi," I said shyly to them both.

Before they had a chance to reply, Debbie's voice rang out. "Dinner's ready, everyone to the dining room!"

The group of us all shuffled to a room attached to the kitchen, and a moment later plates and dishes laden with all sorts of food – pot roast, mashed potatoes, green beans, gravy – flew around us toward the table. I covered my head with my hands instinctively, not wanting to get hit by an errant dish after the morning's adventures, but the food all landed without so much as a spilt drop of gravy, and the whole family sat down to eat.

"So, tell us about your life," Leanne said as she passed me the bowl of mashed potatoes. "Where did your dad take you when your mom died?"

"San Francisco," I explained. "I just graduated from San Francisco State University with a degree in English literature. I'm not going to lie, though, I'm not entirely sure what I want to do with my life. Dad thought I should go to college, and I always enjoyed reading, so I majored in English Literature, but I'm just not sure where I'm going from here. I fell into a bit of a funk after Dad died."

"Well, if you'd like, we can always use an extra pair of hands at the coffee shop," Bob said, looking at Aunt Debbie, who nodded.

"Absolutely. No pressure, of course. If you'd rather find something else in town, or even spend some time just getting used to life here without the pressures of working, we have no problem with that at all. We'll support you for as long as you need."

"Thanks," I said with a grateful smile. "I think I would like to get into the workforce, though. Hopefully this job will go better than my last one. So you manage a coffee shop?"

"It's a coffee shop and roaster," Uncle Bob replied. "It's the family business, although we don't all work there. Debbie and I manage the place, with me taking care of the roasting side of things, distribution to other coffee shops, and all. Debbie manages the retail side of things."

"And they won't let me work there because apparently I'm a hazard," Aunt Lucy replied.

"That's right," Aunt Debbie said, giving her sister the side-eye. "You are absolutely not to be trusted in any customer service-oriented role."

I laughed as my cousins chimed in. "I work there as a barista and server," Leanne said.

"And I do most of the baking," Kaillie added. "It's nice; I've inherited mom's ability to use magic in my cooking, although I have to be careful not to let any of it seep into my cooking at all. I can't be using magic on humans without them knowing about it."

"I'd love to have you working with me at the counter," Leanne said, and I smiled.

"Alright, well, I can't say no to that. I can start tomorrow if that works."

"Perfect," Leanne said excitedly, clapping her hands together. "I can't wait!"

"Well, I must say, I'm looking forward to it as well," Debbie said, beaming at me. "I can't believe you're here. Honestly, I thought this day would never come. A part of me thought Lucy had messed up the tracking spell before you were taken away. It had just been so long, I thought that surely if the tracker had been placed properly you'd have accidentally accessed your powers at some point."

"Hey!" Aunt Lucy replied, lobbing a green bean at her sister. "I might be a lot of things, but bad at magic is not one of them."

"Did you honestly just throw a bean at me?" Debbie replied. "What are you, five years old? No, scratch that, Kaillie was better behaved than this when she was five."

"That's because Kaillie has a stick up her butt about being a good girl," Aunt Lucy replied, with a wink directed at me.

"One of us has to care about this family's reputation," Kaillie replied.

"So," I said, turning to Aunt Lucy. "If everyone else in the family works for the coffee company, what do you do?"

"I wreak havoc and chaos in the town in my own good time," Aunt Lucy deadpanned.

"She's only half kidding," Leanne replied. "Dad had

the news stations on all day today just to make sure there wasn't an infestation of flying frogs appearing out of nowhere somewhere else in the country when he heard Aunt Lucy left to find you."

I laughed. "Only flying donuts, don't worry. And honestly, I'm glad she was there. I had a mall security guard threatening to call the cops on me."

"Well, it sounds like you're truly part of this family, then," Leanne said, digging into her pot roast. "I'm really glad you're here."

The longer I spent with these people, the gladder I was, too.

CHAPTER 6

I woke up the next day feeling like I had been hit by a truck, but I supposed that was to be expected after the tumult of emotions I'd gone through the day before. Still, I rolled out of bed when the alarm went off, yawned, and got dressed. I had messed up my first day on the job once, I was not about to do it again a second time. Especially not when my two bosses were now my aunt and uncle, and they had been so welcoming to me.

A part of me still felt guilty feeling so warmly toward these people. After all, Dad had left Enchanted Enclave for a reason, and he had obviously not wanted my mom's family to be in my life. And yet he'd only been dead a few months and here I was going against one of his strongest wishes in the world. He had also not wanted me to know I was a witch. And again, here

I was, living in a house owned by a woman who made casserole dishes fly through the air like it was nothing.

But at the same time I knew Dad always felt bad about the fact that I had no family growing up. I had often seen him looking longingly at the large families surrounding some of my classmates at Christmas concerts, and he apologized every Thanksgiving when it was just the two of us around the table. His parents had died young, and he was an only child, so the two of us were alone in the world.

At least, that was what he had told me. I wasn't entirely sure what was real anymore, and what wasn't. So I reassured myself with the thought that maybe Dad would be ok with it if I found this side of the family now that he was gone, because otherwise, I really would have been all alone out there.

I didn't resent him for hiding my mom's side of the family from me. I knew he would have done it to protect me. Dad had always been trying to protect me. He didn't want me knowing about these magical powers I apparently had – I was still coming to terms with it, and a part of my brain still refused to believe it was real – and frankly, I could understand that.

It was going to be a big change.

I made my way downstairs to find Aunt Debbie getting ready to go. "Oh good, you're up," she said to me with a smile. "Are you all set? Do you have a jacket?"

I shook my head. "No. I have a sweatshirt upstairs, though."

"Well, grab that," she told me. "You don't live in San Francisco anymore."

A moment later, when I made my way back down the stairs and outside, I realized Aunt Debbie was completely right. Whereas San Francisco in March was generally cool in the mornings, this was colder. A low fog gave the tall fir trees around us an eerie feel, and the house was so isolated I couldn't see the nearest neighbor.

Aunt Debbie unlocked the car in the driveway, a white SUV, and I climbed into the passenger seat next to her.

"So how many people live on Enchanted Enclave, anyway?" I asked. "I think I've heard of it. It's a big tourism destination, right?"

"That's right," Aunt Debbie said with a nod. "We have a permanent population of around five, maybe six thousand people now. We get hundreds of thousands of tourists a year though, mostly in the summer months. It's the slow season right now."

She pulled out of the driveway and down a long, tree-lined dirt road. I looked up in awe as the sun's rays began to peek through the fog, evaporating it on contact.

"Are a lot of the people who live here witches and wizards?"

"Oh no," Aunt Debbie replied. "In fact, it's just us. As

far as I'm aware, we're the only family in the entire human world with magical powers."

I gaped at her. "Seriously? How does that work?"

Debbie shifted uncomfortably in the seat next to her. "I suppose Lucy didn't tell you, then."

"Didn't tell me what?"

"There's another world out there somewhere. A world that can only be accessed by paranormals – witches, wizards, elves, vampires, shifters and fairies. I've never been, and neither has anyone else in the family, because we were kicked out. Some generations ago a member of the Marcet family tried to overthrow the entire paranormal government. They were stopped, and banished to the human world forever along with all of their descendants. From then on, anyone with our blood has been banned from the paranormal world. No paranormals willingly live here, so we're quite isolated."

"Oh," was all I thought to reply. "So we're the outcasts of the magical world?"

"That's right. Please don't think that we're evil at all. It was my great-great-great-grandmother who caused all the trouble, almost two hundred years ago. But memories are long in the paranormal world, especially when vampires and elves live immortal lives, and our family has not been forgiven. At least we were allowed to keep our powers. We still call on Saturn to use our magic, and still belong to that coven."

"Are we allowed to use our magic in front of

people? Other people, I mean. The ones who can't use magic."

"We're not supposed to," Aunt Debbie replied. "It's absolutely frowned upon, and if we do it too much, to the point where we draw attention to ourselves, I'm sure we'll hear from the officials in the paranormal world. They may punish us further, including my limiting our family's access to magic completely."

"Ok," I said. "That's good to know. But, so there's no one I have to tell about my broom ride yesterday, and that it was an accident?"

"No," Aunt Debbie said, shaking her head. "The thing about regular people is that they don't *expect* magic to exist. If they come across it here or there they'll come up with any reason under the sun for the occurrence before they settle on magic."

"That's true," I said. "That was my own reaction yesterday."

"See?" Aunt Debbie said to me with a smile. "Don't worry. I know things are changing for you right now, and you're in the middle of what must be the most confusing period of your life since you hit puberty, but we're here to help you and to guide you through it all. I promise."

"Thanks," I replied warmly. "So how do you know this paranormal world exists, if it's been hundreds of years since we've been exiled from there?"

"There are a few paranormals who are aware of our

existence and come here from time to time. I'm sure you'll meet one or two of them eventually."

"Is there any chance of us ever getting access to that world again?" I asked, and Aunt Debbie shrugged.

"I genuinely don't have a clue. I've never bothered asking about it. Frankly, I've lived my entire life on Enchanted Enclave, and I don't particularly feel the need to see what's behind the curtain, so to speak. I enjoy life here enough that I don't seek more. I hope you will, too."

We had reached what was obviously the main street in town. The double-wide lanes, with extra space for diagonal parking were lined on either side by one and two-story old-style brick buildings, giving the whole street a real charming old-world feel. The streetlamps were in the same olden style, and Aunt Debbie eventually pulled up in front of one of the larger buildings. Made of red brick, with large windows at the front, the black sign hanging above the door read 'Cackling Witch Coffee' in modern white lettering, along with the brand's minimalist logo, a simple white witch's hat above the company name.

Aunt Debbie opened the front door, and I found Leanne already behind the counter. She gave me a quick wave.

"Hey, Eliza," she greeted. "What do you think?"

I looked around, and I had to admit, I was impressed. The space was incredibly spacious, with high ceilings and ample space between the tables and chairs. The walls were exposed brick, with gorgeous nature-themed artwork breaking up the monotony of the pattern. The large windows at the front of the building let a copious amount of light stream in. Leanne was behind the counter on the far side of the room. A refrigerated display case showed off the day's baked goods, while a chalkboard high on the wall above displayed the permanent drink menu. Immediately behind Leanne were windows that looked directly into the roasting side of the business, where large black machines and hessian bags full of beans waiting to be roasted showed off the freshness of the beans customers were drinking.

"This looks amazing," I said truthfully. The space was warm and inviting, and I could absolutely see myself back when I was a student spending multiple hours here working, perhaps at the large, live-edge table in the center of the room, so big it had space for over a dozen chairs.

"Glad you like it," Leanne said. "Now, come on over here, I'll show you how the point of sale works. I figure I'll let you get used to that before teaching you how to use the espresso machine. Now, have you ever worked in a café like this before?"

I shook my head as Aunt Debbie made her way through a set of swinging doors on the far left side of the café that I assumed led to the kitchen. Leanne motioned me over and I spent about fifteen minutes going through her instructions, until finally, a customer walked in.

"Come on, this one's all you," Leanne said. "You've got this. I'm right here in case you screw it up, so don't worry."

Well, it wasn't the world's most traditional pep talk, but I was comforted by the fact that my cousin was ready to take over in case I happened to be the world's worst order-taker as well as a failure as a receptionist.

I smiled at my first customer, a short woman with red hair that reached her waist, wearing a long skirt and a puffy jacket. "Hi there. How can I help you today?"

"Yes, could I please get a double-shot latte made with almond milk?" the woman asked. I nodded and wrote the order down on a sticky note, placing it on the coffee machine where Leanne had instructed me to do so. I quickly found the button for 'latte' in the iPad's point-of-sale system, chose the almond milk add-on, and gave the woman her total.

"Here you go," she said to me as she handed me a five. "Are you new in town? I don't recognize you."

"I am," I replied as I handed her a few coins in change. "My name's Eliza; I'm a long-lost cousin to Leanne here. I just moved back to the area from San Francisco."

"Oh, welcome," the woman replied. "I'm Janice. I'm an artist; those are some of my paintings on the wall. I also run one of the yoga studios here in town."

"They're gorgeous," I said earnestly. "I love the one of the mother bear with her two cubs."

"Why thank you," Janice replied as Leanne handed her a cup of coffee. "I appreciate you saying so. I'm sure I'll see you around."

She held her cup up in salute and made her way out the door. As soon as it closed behind her I let out a breath I hadn't realized I'd been holding. I had done it! I had successfully helped a customer without causing chaos and almost getting arrested.

"See?" Leanne said to me with a wink. "Nothing to it."

CHAPTER 7

With my confidence at an all-time high after serving a handful of customers without incident I greeted an older gentleman who came in shortly after nine in the morning with a wide smile. Leanne had gone to the back to get an extra plate of muffins to replace the blueberry ones we'd already sold out of, and told me to give her a shout when she was needed to make coffee.

"Hi there, what can I get for you today?"

"Coffee," the man replied. "This *is* a coffee shop, isn't it?"

"Absolutely, what kind of coffee can I get you?"

The man sighed dramatically. "Just a normal coffee. Oh, and a donut."

Just a normal coffee. That was fine; that had to mean a brewed coffee. "What size would you like?"

"Normal size, geez. I don't come in here in the morning to be asked a million questions."

A blush crawled up my face. This man was *rude*, and to be honest, I wasn't quite sure what to do. We didn't have a "normal" sized coffee cup, so I poured him a medium, which seemed to be what he was after, as he didn't complain about it when I put it in front of him.

"For the donut, is chocolate glazed ok?" I asked, looking at the small selection in the display cabinet.

"Sure, whatever," the man replied. I rang up his total and he looked at me closely. "You're new here, aren't you? I don't recognize you at all."

"That's right," I said cheerily. "I just moved here from San Francisco."

The man grunted. "Stupid city folk. Come up here looking for a change in scenery without really understanding what life here is all about. Well, I hope you realize soon enough that it's not all about doing yoga in the woods and you go back to your life sitting at a computer all day."

I was so taken aback by the man's nasty attitude that I physically took a step back. "Excuse me, but that's not my situation at all. I've just lost my father, and I've moved here to be closer to the rest of my family."

"Oh, don't tell me you're one of the Marcets."

"That's right, Patricia was my mother."

The man grunted. "Great. Another Marcet. That's just what this town needs. Well, as long as you make coffee like the rest of them and keep to yourself, it can't be too bad."

Without another word, he grabbed the donut off the counter and headed to a seat in the corner, leaving me practically speechless at the counter.

I wasn't so green that I was completely unaware of rude customers in retail – friends of mine in college who had worked for a living were full of horror stories – but it was another thing entirely when it happened to you.

Leanne came back from the kitchen and I motioned toward the man with my head. "Who's that?"

As soon as she saw him, Leanne scowled. "Ugh. Sorry you had to deal with him. Leonard Steele. He's the town grouch. He's worked security at the bank at night since before I was born. It's basically the only job he's good for, since it's one of the few in town that doesn't involve any interaction with other human beings, which is perfect for him."

I laughed. "Yeah, that's kind of the impression I got. He told me I was a city person and I should go back there, and that our family is good for nothing."

"That sounds about right," Leanne said. "Just ignore him. Despite his complaining about how terrible our family is, he does come in basically every day for a coffee. His shift ends at nine in the morning, when the bank opens, and he comes in before heading home and sleeping."

"Ok," I said, making a mental note of the information. Who knew, maybe over time I would win Leonard over and convince him that I wasn't an awful person because I moved here from the city and because I was a part of this family. What on earth could he have against the family, anyway?

Before I had a chance to ask Leanne that question, though, Leonard began to cough violently. I grabbed a carafe of water and made my way over to him with a glass. Was he choking on a piece of his donut? He thumped his chest a few times, and panic rushed through me as I realized this wasn't just a sip of coffee that went down the wrong way. This was serious!

"Does anyone here know the Heimlich?" I called out, and a woman rushed over. She made her way behind Leonard and grabbed him around the middle, pressing firmly a few times, but nothing happened. Eventually, he passed out, and I raced back to the counter to grab my phone only to find Leanne already using it to call 9-1-1. The woman immediately began doing CPR on him, but after a moment, she checked his pulse and shook her head, leaning back on her heels.

"I'm afraid there's nothing we can do. This man is dead."

"Dead?" I gasped, a hand flying to my mouth. "Did he choke?"

The woman looked curious. "I don't know. If everyone who's in here now wouldn't mind staying for a little while longer, the police are going to have to come and question everyone."

I made my way over to her. "You seem to know how things are done around here."

"Nancy Gerard," she said, holding a hand out to me. "I'm one of the nurses at the hospital here in town."

"Nice to meet you, though obviously not under these circumstances."

Nancy nodded. "Can you lock up the front doors? I don't want anyone else getting in here."

"Of course," I replied, instantly making my way over and doing as Nancy asked, flipping the "open" sign to "closed" while I was at it.

"Coffee is on us while we're waiting for the ambulance to get here," Leanne announced to everyone waiting, and a couple of people made their way to the counter while I went into the kitchen at the back, where I found Debbie and Kaillie poring over a certain recipe.

"Hi, Eliza," Debbie said to me. "How are things going out there? Nothing too stressful, I hope?"

I had no idea how to break it to her. I decided to be straight. "Well, um, someone died."

"What do you mean?"

"As in, he started choking, and Nancy Gerard tried to do the Heimlich on him, and then she did CPR, but she said he was dead."

The color drained from Debbie and Kaillie's faces.

"You're joking," Kaillie said.

"I wish I was," I replied. "Debbie, it's probably a good idea for you to come out and handle things. I've locked the front door and closed the coffee shop, and Leanne is making everyone free coffee while we wait for the paramedics to arrive, but, um…"

I didn't really know how to finish off the sentence, but Debbie sprang into action. "Absolutely. Good job handling the situation without me, but I will come out."

Kaillie looked like she was going to faint, so as Debbie made her way out to the main part of the coffee shop, I stayed with her.

"Are you alright?" I asked, and Kaillie nodded.

"Yeah. Thanks for asking. I don't do very well with situations like this. I always think of the fact that we were exiled, and how our family is known in the paranormal world for being awful, and now something like this happens in our shop. It's just bad news."

"Hey," I said, making my way toward her. "This isn't our fault. It's no one in this family's fault, ok? Leonard probably just had a heart attack or something. Or he choked. But there's no way it was anything unnatural."

Kaillie nodded. "That's good, at least. I'm just always worried that one day we're going to do something over-the-top. I just wish everyone in the paranormal world would realize that we're not terrible people, and that they'd let us go back there. I wish I could be a part of a normal coven like everyone else. Whenever anything out of the ordinary happens to us I'm always reminded that we're outcasts, even if it has nothing to do with us."

"I hope you get to visit the paranormal world one day," I said to her. "But don't worry. I'm sure everything will be fine."

Little did I know just how wrong I was.

CHAPTER 8

I left the kitchen area and made my way back to the main coffee shop right as the paramedics and police arrived.

My life flashed back to dad's heart attack, and how almost the exact same scene had unfolded. I steadied myself against a nearby table as the professionals went about the job. Leonard's body had been covered up by a blanket that must have been procured from somewhere, and the customers who were in the building at the time had moved to the other side of the room.

I made my way to Leanne and Debbie behind the counter.

"Does he have a wife?"

"No," she said, shaking her head. "Leonard is single. Was single. His only family in town is his brother, Roman."

Just then one of the police officers made his way

toward us. He was tall, with brown hair that he kept having to brush out of his eyes. His lips were plump and round, and his brown eyes were kind and gentle. When he smiled, dimples appeared in his cheeks.

"Excuse me, ladies," he greeted us. "I'm wondering if there's a private place where I might be able to interview people alone."

"Of course, you can use the kitchen," Debbie said, motioning for him to follow her. "My daughter Kaillie is in there right now baking, but I'll have her come out here instead."

"Thank you," he replied, following after Debbie.

"I wonder why he needs to speak to everyone," Leanne said, her eyes trailing him. "Maybe it's not as innocent as it seems. Maybe someone murdered Leonard."

"Don't say that!" I hissed. "Who would have murdered him, anyway?"

Leanne shrugged. "Half the town, if given the chance, would be my guess. He was a cranky old man and I don't think I've ever heard a single good thing said about him."

"There's a difference between thinking someone is cranky and annoying and murdering them," I pointed out. "Besides, he was sitting in that corner ever since he ordered the coffee. If someone murdered him, it means that someone was in the coffee shop."

"Oh yeah, I guess I didn't think of that," Leanne said.

"Well, I'm sure you're right. It's probably nothing. He was old, after all."

"Yeah," I said. Still, I felt bad for his brother. The loss of my father was still so acute that I really empathized with anyone else going through this same sort of situation. Kaillie came out from the kitchen a moment later, her face pale.

"I can't believe it."

"Hey, it's going to be ok," I said, reassuring her. "Why don't you take a seat at one of the tables, and I'll get you a cup of tea."

Kaillie nodded, and Leanne showed me how to get the hot water from the coffee machine into a cup. I added a teabag and took it to my cousin, sitting across from her. "I know it's stressful, but it's going to be fine. It's an unfortunate accident."

"Yeah, but why did it have to happen here? I know that sounds callous, but I can't help but think that it's because of our family."

"You really feel bad about the fact that we're not allowed into this so-called paranormal world, don't you?"

Kaillie nodded. "It's just hard to grow up knowing you're an outcast, I think. I know I'm technically a member of the coven of Saturn, but I don't feel like I really have a coven. There's only the family. I feel like if we were allowed to live with everyone else there would be more of a community feel, and I really wish we had that. We're never going to, I know, but a part of me hopes that maybe if I show that we're not as bad as everyone in the paranormal world seems to think we are, one day they'll let us back in."

I smiled at her, although to be honest, I couldn't really relate. Growing up, it had always been just Dad and me, and that had been fine with me. I hadn't needed any more. It was the two of us against the world, and that was all I needed. I thought we would have had that for a little bit longer. Still, I felt bad for Kaillie. I imagined it must have been difficult for her, wanting to be a part of something bigger, and not being allowed to be a part of it.

"You're a good person," I told her.

"I try to be."

"Look, I know I can't change anything about what the other witches think. But your family seems to be pretty good."

She barked out a laugh. "With one glaring exception."

"Aunt Lucy?" I asked, and Kaillie nodded.

"That's right. She and her friends – she calls them Lucy's Floozies because of course she does – are always going around getting into trouble. It drives me crazy. Why she can't just work hard and keep her head down like the rest of us is beyond me."

"Well, some people just aren't wired that way."

"I hope that one day the people in the coven see that we're not awful and we're let back in," Kaillie said. "But it's hard when you don't know what kind of information they're getting. That's why I'm so upset about Leonard dying here. I know it was just a coincidence, but what if they don't know that in the magical world? What if they think we killed him, or think we had something to do with his death? Then we'll never be let in."

"I'm sure they're not getting their information in drips and drabs. After all, these people are witches and wizards. They'll have ways of getting the whole story, I'm sure."

"I hope so," Kaillie said with a sigh. "Look at me here, whining about my own problems, when I'm sure all of this must be the strangest conversation ever."

"It's certainly been… interesting," I replied. "Honestly, I woke up today and a part of me thought I'd dreamt the entire thing. It doesn't seem real, and yet the longer this goes on, the more I'm having to accept that it is."

I received a sympathetic smile in reply. "It must be strange. It was always so funny growing up, while everyone was reading *Harry Potter* and pretending magic was real, we always had to hide the fact that we had real magical powers. I guess you're getting to live your own real adventure now."

"Yeah," I replied. "It's a lot more confusing than it is in books, though." The fact that Dad hadn't wanted me to know I had magical powers was really something. I wished I knew why. And yet I was never going to get that opportunity.

Tears sprung to my eyes, but I blinked them back. Just then, Debbie came out from the kitchen at the back and made her way toward us.

"Eliza, he'd like to talk to you," she told me, putting a comforting hand on my shoulder. I stood up and made my way to kitchen at the back, where I found the policeman looking over the notes he had written in a small pad. He smiled at me when I came in and motioned for me to sit on a small bench near a stainless steel table.

"Hi, I'm Detective Ross Andrews," he said, holding out a hand. "I don't believe we've met."

"Eliza Emory," I replied, reaching forward to shake his hand. As soon as my skin touched his, a spark of electricity flew through me. Ok, so this guy was good-looking, and I hadn't had a boyfriend – or heck, even a one-night stand – in far too long. I smiled, pretending nothing had happened, and sat down on the bench.

"So you're new in town?" he asked, and I nodded.

"Just moved here yesterday, actually. I lived in San Francisco, but my dad died a few months ago and now my only family live here."

"I'm sorry," Detective Andrews replied.

"Thanks."

"So this is your first day working at Cackling Witch Coffee?"

I nodded. "That's right. My Aunt Debbie and Uncle Robert were nice enough to offer me a job here. I just started this morning."

"Did you know the victim, Leonard Steele?"

"No," I replied. "I mean, I served him his coffee and donut, of course. But I had no idea who he was."

"What did you think of him?" Detective Andrews asked, and I couldn't help but think I noticed a flitter of a smile on his lips.

I shrugged. "Honestly, he didn't seem like the nicest person. But being mean doesn't mean a person deserves to die. It can lead to health issues though, and I guess his heart just couldn't take it anymore."

"What makes you think it was a heart attack?"

I was taken aback by the question. "Well, I mean, it was so quick," I said. "And he started by coughing, and thumping his chest. Honestly, I thought he had choked on something, but then Nancy did the Heimlich on him, and she's a nurse. You would think that if he had choked, she would have gotten it out. So it had to be his heart."

Detective Andrews nodded slowly. "Ok. After you served him, did you see anyone else approach Leonard?"

I scrunched my brows together as I tried to think back. "Honestly, I'm not really sure. I think a woman came over and spoke to him for a second. He also got up and went to the bathroom at one point. I don't know if he saw anyone in there, obviously."

"Do you remember seeing anyone near Leonard's drink when he left it unattended?"

My eyes widened. "You don't mean-"

"I don't mean anything at the moment, no," Detective Andrews interrupted with a kind smile. "These are just ordinary questions, par for the course in any investigation. Don't worry."

His words did little to put my mind at ease. Would he really be asking things like that if he didn't suspect foul play?

"I honestly don't know," I replied with a shrug. "It's my first day on the job, I was trying to figure out how everything worked, and once I served Leonard he stopped being my focus. Leanne might have noticed a little bit more."

"She would be your... cousin, right? Leanne Stevens?"

"That's right. I guess this is a small town," I said with a smile.

Detective Andrews grinned. "I went to school with Leanne; she was a couple of years younger than me. But yeah, you'll find most people around here are pretty tight. Is there anything else you can think of that might help?"

I shook my head. "Sorry, I don't. I do want to ask though – what do you think happened?"

Detective Andrews shrugged. "I do my best not to rush to any conclusions. The medical examiner is coming over from the mainland and will have a look at the body, and I'll trust what she says. Would you mind asking Leanne to come in, please?"

I nodded and left the kitchen, my mind whirling with thoughts.

"Detective Andrews wants to speak to you," I said to Leanne as I made my way back to the counter. She let out a giggle.

"Detective Andrews. It sounds so professional. Up until about two months ago he was just Officer Andrews, handing out speeding tickets. Thanks."

She made her way toward the kitchen at the back and I stole another look at Kaillie, doing my best to avoid the scene nearby. She still looked a bit more pale than usual, but a bit of color was coming back to her face.

I really hoped she was right, but I couldn't help but feel a little bit more worried than I had before the chat with Detective Andrews. Maybe things weren't so cut-and-dried after all.

CHAPTER 9

About an hour later, when Detective Andrews had spoken to everyone in the coffee shop we were all finally given permission to leave. The group of customers couldn't wait to get out of there, and shortly thereafter the only non-law enforcement officials left in the building were Debbie, Leanne, Kaillie and me.

"Why don't you girls head on out?" Debbie suggested. "I'm going to stay here in case I'm needed for anything."

Figuring that was probably a good idea, the three of us left and made our way down the street.

"Did you get the distinct impression Detective Andrews thought it was a murder after all?" Leanne asked me, and I nodded.

"Yeah, I did."

Kaillie let out a moan. "I knew it. I just knew it.

Someone's been murdered and it was in our coffee shop. The coven is going to think one of us did it."

"Don't be ridiculous," Leanne replied. "Obviously it wasn't one of us. None of us had any access to his food and drink, anyway." She stopped and bit her lip as she realized that wasn't true – I had been the one to serve him.

"Well, at least I don't have a motive?" I offered with a shrug. "I didn't even know the guy. No one can think I murdered someone randomly the first time I met him, right?"

"That's right," Leanne said. "So there you have it. Even if he was killed, no one is going to think it was Eliza. There are no problems at all."

Kaillie didn't look convinced.

"Come on," Leanne said. "None of us have had lunch and it's almost two, I'm starving. Let's show Eliza the best place in town for a good lunch."

Otterly Delicious was a small diner-like restaurant, not quite the sort of place that had tablecloths. Everyone seemed to order from the large counter at the front, and food was then brought to a chosen table. As the smell of food wafted toward my nostrils I realized what a good idea this had been; my stomach grumbled in anticipation. I was starving.

I settled on the macaroni and cheese with a side of tomato soup, and the three of us found a table near the window where we could watch people walking past.

"I still can't believe this happened," Kaillie moaned. "They're never going to let us into the magical world now."

"Hey, there's literally nothing I can ever do to get invited," Leanne replied. "At least you've got a chance. And the ability to use magic. Why couldn't you just use a spell to see if that guy was dead?"

Kaillie gasped. "Use magic in public? Absolutely not. That goes against every rule the paranormal world has."

"Well, maybe they shouldn't have kicked the family out if they didn't want magic to be used around us normal humans," Leanne suggested with a shrug. "Personally, if I had magical powers, I'd be using them all the time. Need to make the bed? Bam. Magic. Forgot my lunch at home? Bam, BLT and fries ready and waiting. Jessica Longview steals my boyfriend again? Bam. Yeast infection."

I snorted with laughter at the thought while Kaillie looked horrified. "You wouldn't be able to use magic like that! You can't use it to make people's lives worse!"

"Aunt Lucy does it all the time," Leanne shot back.

"Aunt Lucy shouldn't be doing that," Kaillie said. "Magic should be used for good, and only good."

"You're such a boring waste of magical powers," Leanne replied. "I wish I'd gotten them instead of you." I watched the exchange with interest, and a moment later a waitress came by with our drinks. I sipped my iced tea, but before Leanne and Kaillie could continue their argument about the proper use of magic, the discussion turned to me.

"So what was your dad like?" Kaillie asked. "I wonder why he didn't want you to know about us."

"I wonder too," I said. "He never liked magic. He didn't stop me from reading books like Harry Potter or Coraline, but I could tell that he didn't like them, either. He was nice. He gave good hugs. And whenever I had a problem, he always worked through it with me. He wasn't the type to tell me to figure it out myself. He would sit me down, and we would get through it together. That was what I liked the most about him; I knew I could go to him about anything."

"Did you get in trouble a lot growing up?" Leanne asked, and I shook my head.

"No. I didn't want to disappoint my dad, so I always did my best to be kind. That was the main value he always tried to instill in me: to be kind. He would always tell me that you never knew what someone else was going through."

"He sounds like a good guy," Leanne said, and the tears welled up in my eyes once more.

"He was. He really was."

Kaillie put her hand on mine and gave it a squeeze, and I returned it. "Thanks. It's still hard to think he's gone. Really hard."

"But he's not gone," Kaillie said softly. "He lives on

in you. Every time you're kind to someone, your father's spirit lives on."

That was an absolutely beautiful way to think about it.

Just then, the waitress came by with our food orders, and I spent the next couple of minutes burying smooth, creamy macaroni and cheese topped with a gorgeous breadcrumb crust into my mouth.

"It's strange thinking about Leonard being gone," Leanne said after a few minutes, staring out the window. "I mean, I knew he was old. Heck, he was already old when we were kids. I'm surprised he was still working, really. But he was such a fixture around town, it's going to be weird not seeing him around anymore."

"He always wrote letters to the paper," Kaillie said. "The editor, Carly, told me once that he always wrote five or six letters, usually complaining about individual people in town, and they never published those ones. But when he wrote one that wasn't profanity-laced they would, and they were always entertaining."

"He did get things done, though," Leanne said with a grin. "Remember the time a couple of years ago when the library cut their hours due to budget cuts? He argued that the library was a place where teenagers could hang out at night rather than drinking in the park, and he actually got so much support that the town was forced to increase the library's budget so they could stay open until ten o'clock."

"Yeah, but then there was also the time when he complained about the grocery store not carrying his favorite brand of cookies anymore, and he had a meltdown that ended with him doing a one-man protest at the front every day for two months."

"Well, he certainly sounded like a character," I said.

"He was," Leanne confirmed. "He did have a lot more enemies than friends, though. Who knows, maybe he would have lived longer if he didn't automatically assume that every person he ever met was awful and that they had to prove otherwise."

"What about his brother? Did he get along with him?" I asked, moving to my soup and taking a careful sip of the hot liquid.

"They used to," Kaillie replied. "They lived together, in their old family home. Since their mom died, though, they haven't gotten along as well as they used to."

"It's a run-down cabin by the water," Leanne explained. "Honestly, I'm kind of surprised the town hasn't condemned it as unlivable; the thing is practically falling down, and every time we get a windstorm that's more than just a small gust, I'm worried the thing will fall over."

"It's not the sturdiest building anymore," Kaillie confirmed. "And I don't think either brother was taking particularly good care of it. But as Leanne said, they both seemed to be content there, so who are we to complain? I always did kind of imagine both of them dying with the house crumbling to pieces over them one day, though."

"Well, if someone *did* kill Leonard, it wasn't Roman," Leanne said. "After all, he wasn't in the coffee shop at all."

"Can you please stop talking like that's what happened?" Kaillie said, looking around furtively. "You're going to have half the town talking about it."

Before I got a chance to ask about the feud between Roman and Leonard, however, the strangest character walked through the front door of Otterly Delightful. He looked around, spotted us, and immediately began making his way over. He was tall, with pointed ears, like one of the elves from *Lord of the Rings*. His face was pale, which contrasted with his dark hair that reached his shoulders, and his blue eyes were like looking into glacier ice.

He sat down at the table next to us and it took everything in my power not to stare at him. Instead, I shoved a spoonful of soup into my mouth, immediately burning my tongue. Great.

Who *was* this?

Kaillie was now sitting straight and tall in her chair, like a student trying to suck up to her teacher.

"Hey, Kyran," Leanne said to him with a nod. "Looking for Aunt Lucy?"

"That's right," the man replied. "There were reports

of excessive and inconspicuous magic used yesterday in the human world."

"And so automatically you thought of our aunt," Leanne said with a smile.

"Naturally."

"Even though California is two states away."

"The fact that you've heard about the magical events makes me think I'm on the right track," Kyran said with a grin, leaning back in his chair.

Leanne shrugged. "Word gets around. I don't know where Lucy is, but she's not here. Anyway, have you met Eliza? She's our long-lost cousin who only found out yesterday that she's a witch. Eliza, this is Kyran. He's an elf."

My eyes widened at the last statement.

"A real elf?" I said in a half-whisper. Kyran laughed.

"Yup, she's new alright."

"Do you live in the magical world we're not allowed in?"

"I do," Kyran replied.

"So it's real. It's not something someone just made up?"

Kyran shook his head. "No, it's definitely real. I'm one of the few paranormals that comes into the human world on a regular basis, though."

"What do you do here?" I asked.

"My role involves basically unofficially being a link between law enforcement in the paranormal world and crime committed by paranormals in the human world.

Sometimes, paranormals come here to do illegal things thinking they'll get away with them more easily than in the paranormal world. My role is to hunt them down and bring them to justice. As a result, I'm often also given messages to pass on, like the one I have for your aunt that she needs to stop using magic in front of humans."

"Oh. Well, that's got to be interesting, at the very least."

"It certainly is," Kyran replied. "Well, I'm going to head off and try to find your aunt. It was nice meeting you, Eliza."

"You too," I said, still kind of shocked at the whole situation. An *elf*? Really?"

I watched his retreating form and then turned to my cousins. "Is he really magical?" I hissed, and Leanne laughed.

"Yeah. Even *he* gets to have magical powers, and I don't. Kyran is a good person. You can trust him. He gives Aunt Lucy tons of crap about using her magic inappropriately, but frankly, she deserves it."

"I hope he knows I'm always responsible in my use of magic," Kaillie added quickly, and Leanne shot her a look.

"Seeing as you try to remind him of it every single time you see him, I can't see how he isn't. But that will have no impact on anything. It's not like Kyran is in charge of anything. He's just the messenger."

"You never know," Kaillie said with a shrug. "It can't

hurt to have as many paranormals as possible aware of the fact that I reject my family's history and am dedicated to being the best witch I can."

I smiled as I dug into the mac and cheese. I was starting to like my cousins.

CHAPTER 10

When we finished eating Leanne leaned back in her chair. We were just getting ready to leave when a familiar face walked through the door: it was Aunt Lucy, followed closely by three other women. Lucy strutted at the front of them like she was their leader. As soon as she saw us she made her way over; it was like a sexagenarian Mean Girls.

"Boy, am I glad to see you," Lucy said, taking the seat Kyran had recently vacated. The other ladies grabbed some chairs and pulled them over to our table. "I heard old Leonard croaked in the middle of the coffee shop today. Why didn't anyone tell me?"

"Because our instinct when someone dies a few feet away isn't to call you straight away," Leanne offered. "We were a little bit busy with other things."

"Well, you know what I've heard," Lucy said, leaning

forward. "Apparently, it wasn't a natural death. Leonard was murdered."

My eyes and Kaillie's widened at the proclamation, but and Leanne looked nonplussed and just crossed her arms.

"Of course you're going to have heard that. This is Enchanted Enclave. Everyone talks. That doesn't make it true."

"Oh, but in this case, it is. Dorothy here's husband works as a police officer, remember? He heard it from his boss. They won't be sure until the tox screen comes back, but Leonard was almost certainly poisoned."

My blood ran cold as I looked over at the woman to Lucy's left whose expression had suddenly gone smug. Her grey hair was cut to her shoulders, her blue eyes framed by wide-rimmed glasses. She seemed like the type of woman who would have had a job working a checkout counter somewhere where she could gossip with people.

"That's right," she said, leaning forward. "Joe told me himself. They don't want anyone to know, of course, so you had better keep this information to yourselves. But I swear it's the truth. The police think Leonard was murdered."

Kaillie and I shared a worried expression, although the cause for worry was different for each of us. I knew Kaillie was scared that the paranormal world would find out what happened and blame our family, but my worries were more self-centered. I had been one of the few people to interact with Leonard at the coffee shop, and I had been the one to serve him both the coffee and the donut. If anyone would have had the opportunity to poison him, it was me.

I had to be the prime suspect in this murder.

That was just great. Yesterday, at my first day on the job I had gone for an accidental joyride on a broom through the middle of a mall. Today, my first day at a new job I was suspected of murdering a customer.

At this rate, by the time I got out of jail and found my next job I was going to accidentally trigger a nuclear explosion.

I tried to keep up with the conversation between Leanne and Lucy, but my brain kept going back to the fact that I was going to be locked up forever. I should never have left San Francisco. I didn't know what to do. Dad would have known. Dad would have told me exactly what I had to do to fix this. Dad would have never let me come here in the first place. Dad never wanted me to know about my mom's family here on Enchanted Enclave, and maybe there was a good reason for that.

I'd messed up by coming here. I didn't blame my family; I was sure they didn't know what was about to happen. There was no way. But the fact was, less than twenty-four hours after I'd moved here, a man had been murdered immediately after I served him. Even though I didn't know him at all and had interacted with him for under two minutes total, there was no getting away from it. I had to be a suspect in his murder.

"Excuse me," I said, standing up from the table. "I'm just going to take a walk."

I didn't wait for a reply before I sped out from the diner and onto the street, blinking back tears. How could this be happening to me? What had I ever done to deserve this?

I knew Leonard had it worse. After all, he was the person who had been murdered. But I was the one who was almost certainly facing life in prison for having done it.

No, I had to stop thinking this way. After all, I was getting *way* ahead of myself here. First of all, it wasn't even confirmed that Leonard had been murdered. It might very well turn out to be a fiction invented by a police officer with an over-active imagination. And even if it did turn out to be a murder, there was no guarantee that I was going to be fingered. After all, I didn't even know the guy.

Breathing in the cool spring afternoon air, I began walking down the main street in town, aimlessly wandering, trying to get my emotions under control.

I shivered slightly as I walked past a gift shop featuring a number of cute little items in the window, and I figured maybe doing a little bit of browsing might get my mind off things.

I stepped into the store, immediately finding my senses overwhelmed by the smell of a display of bath bombs near the front door. They smelled like eight hundred grandmothers had poured their entire bags of toiletries on the floor. It wouldn't have been an unpleasant smell if there were just a couple of bath bombs on display, but this was truly overwhelming, and not in a good way.

Moving past the bath bombs and away from the smell, I found myself heading toward a display of pillows embroidered with pictures of woodland creatures. Adorable deer, fox, squirrels, otters, beavers and more were all artfully added to pillows which read 'Enchanted Enclave' in the corner. If I had come here as a tourist and actually had money to spend, I would have snatched up these pillows in a heartbeat.

"They're just gorgeous, aren't they?" a voice said from behind me, and I turned around to find myself looking at a tall woman who looked to be in her late fifties. Her appearance was obviously of the upmost importance to her, with her hair styled well, and her makeup flawless. Her face was plastered with the smile of a typical saleswoman, but it fell as soon as she saw me.

"Oh. You're Lucy's new niece, aren't you? I heard you came back to town. Patricia and Daniel's daughter."

"That's right," I said with a nod. "Eliza Emory." I held out a hand matched with a friendly smile, and the woman took it, but the split second of hesitation before she did told me she already wasn't my biggest fan. I was half surprised she didn't wipe her hand on her pants when she was finished.

"What brings you to town then? That's just what we need, another Marcet family member running around. I heard you've already managed to murder poor old Leonard. He might have been a bit cantankerous from time to time, but I'm sure he didn't do anything to deserve what you did to him."

Her eyes narrowed at me and I stepped back from shock. This woman was actually accusing me of having killed Leonard. And to my face!

"I didn't kill him," I said quickly. "I swear, I didn't. I don't know what happened. He was just eating and drinking, and then he started coughing, and next thing I knew he was dead."

"Like I'm going to believe anyone related to Lucy Marcet. Your whole family is bad news, and I'm sure you're no exception. Who leaves Enchanted Enclave to go live elsewhere? Only people with something to hide. Now, I know you're new here, so let me give you some advice: leave. You've been here for one day and you've already caused irreparable damage to the fabric of this community by killing one of its stalwarts. Get off this island, and go live somewhere else where you and your crazy family are actually wanted. And do us all a favor and take Lucy with you, will you?"

I gaped at the woman. How could one human being be so mean to another? She had just reignited all of the fears I'd convinced myself weren't real. Here I was, having a local small business owner telling me to leave because she thought I was a killer.

Tears threatened to sting my eyes, but I blinked them back. I didn't know who this woman was, but I wasn't going to give her the satisfaction of seeing me cry. Not a chance.

"Well, if this is how you treat all the customers to your shop, I'm surprised you're still in business," I replied as politely as I could muster. "I'm obviously not welcome here, so I'm going to leave."

"You're not welcome in the whole town," the woman spat. "You're a killer. We don't like people from the city, especially not when they go around murdering our citizens."

I didn't reply and just left the shop, trying to get to the end of the street before I let the tears fall. Luckily, this not being peak tourist season, the road was practically deserted. I followed it aimlessly, and about three minutes after the row of shops had finished, the road ended at the entrance to a short trail that led to a beach.

The ocean waves pounded the shore as the wind picked up. I sat on a piece of driftwood, holding my arms close to me as the cold air hit my skin, and cried. The wind drowned out the sound of my sobbing as I thought about how lost I was without Dad.

"What do I do?" I asked him, my voice immediately carried away by the gusts. "What am I supposed to do?"

Dad always had an answer for me. He was the one

person in this world that I could always rely on, and yet, he was gone.

The emptiness that filled me was all-encompassing. I sobbed harder, ugly crying as my shoulders heaved and my nose ran, letting the emotions I'd been keeping pent up flow freely. I missed my dad so much. What would he have done? What would he have suggested? What was I supposed to do?

I could always run. I could take a ferry back to the mainland – was there a bridge? I really didn't know much about this island. But there had to be a way to get back to Seattle, and then I could fly back to San Francisco. I didn't even have to go back there. I could go anywhere in the country, or anywhere in the world. I was completely alone, after all. I could start all over somewhere else.

And yet, at the same time, a part of me didn't want to leave. After all, I did like Leanne and Kaillie, and Aunt Debbie was really nice. Even Aunt Lucy was a little bit strange, but she had saved me from the security guard. And Uncle Bob was the first to offer me the new job. I was sure he had no idea I was going to be accused of murder on my first day.

They were nice people. They were all nice to me, and a part of me wanted to stay and get to know them better. They weren't my dad, and I wasn't close to them yet, but I imagined over time maybe I could be. But if I chose to go that route, it would mean having to stay here at Enchanted Enclave. And that meant figuring out a solution to the current problem.

Then, a moment later, it hit me.

Everyone in this town thought I was a killer. And if I thought about it, I couldn't exactly blame them. I had come in, and then less than twenty-four hours later Leonard had been killed, after I had served him his food and drink. I had the opportunity, and as an outsider, I was obviously a suspect.

But someone out there really had done it, really *had* killed Leonard. Who was it? If I could find that person, and prove that they had done it, then I would be off the hook.

I had to solve this murder and prove to everyone in town that I was just a normal new arrival from the city, and that I intended to make Enchanted Enclave my permanent home.

I had a plan. Now, I just had to figure out how to put it in place.

"I love you, Dad," I whispered into the wind before turning around and making my way back into town.

CHAPTER 11

"I invited your cousins over for dinner again," Aunt Debbie said when I made my way back home. It turned out it wasn't too difficult to find; the island was smaller than I thought and the waitress who had served us at Otterly Delicious was happy to give me directions when I made my way back to Main Street. "I hope that's alright with you. I thought you'd enjoy having some company your own age."

"Thanks," I said gratefully. "I really like them."

"I'm very glad to hear it," Aunt Debbie replied. "I know it wasn't the ideal first day for you in town, and I understand if you don't want to continue working at the coffee shop, but obviously if you're still up to it we'd love to have you keep working there."

I considered her words for a moment. "Well, it can't get worse than today, can it?" I asked.

Aunt Debbie gave me a sympathetic look as she

dumped a carton of spaghetti into a boiling pot. "Leonard's death wasn't foreseeable. We all know it wasn't your fault."

Just then, the front door opened and Kaillie's voice called through the house. "Mom! We're here!"

"In the kitchen," Aunt Debbie called out and my two cousins appeared in the doorway a moment later.

"Hey," Leanne said to me with a quick nod.

"Are you alright?" Kaillie asked. "You left the diner pretty quickly."

"Yeah, I didn't mean to alarm you. I was just a bit overwhelmed after learning Leonard was murdered."

Leanne nodded. "It's all over town now. Turns out it's true. He really was killed."

Kaillie shook her head. "I can't believe it."

"I went into one of the gift shops to look at some stuff, and the woman who owned it practically accused me of the murder. She said the last thing this town needs is another Marcet, or something along those lines."

Leanne blew a raspberry. "That's Ariadne. Ariadne Stewart. If anyone in town deserves to be murdered, it's her."

"Leanne!" Debbie scolded from her spot in front of the oven.

"What? It's true," Leanne replied with a shrug. "Ariadne and Aunt Lucy grew up together. They've hated each other since high school, although don't ask me what started it. Aunt Lucy says Ariadne started it, but frankly I'm not sure I believe her. Anyway, the two of them have hated each other since the dawn of time. Don't take anything she says personally; she hates you for your relatives, not for you yourself."

"Well, I guess that's a relief, in a way," I muttered.

"Hello! Dinner better be ready, I'm starving," a familiar voice called from the hall, and a moment later Aunt Lucy strutted through the doorway, immediately making her way to the stove to see what Aunt Debbie had cooking.

"Wait until it's served like everyone else," Aunt Debbie scolded.

"When you get to my age, you need to take advantage of every second you can," Aunt Lucy replied. "You said dinner was going to be ready at six, and it's just after six."

"So does Aunt Lucy live here as well?" I asked, and Aunt Debbie nodded.

"She needs adult supervision at all times," Leanne laughed, earning herself a glare from my aunt.

"Rather, the idea that Debbie has to live all by herself in this enormous house is just too much for me to bear, so I moved in to keep her company after Kaillie moved out. I'm unselfish like that. My room is on the other side of the house from yours, though, Eliza, so you wouldn't have seen me last night."

"Hey Aunt Lucy, Eliza ran into Ariadne today."

Lucy narrowed her eyes as she looked at me. "Was she nice to you? She better have been nice."

"Umm, not exactly," I replied cautiously.

"I'll have her taken care of," Lucy said simply.

"Do *not* hex her," Aunt Debbie warned, waving the wooden spoon she had been stirring the meat sauce with in Aunt Lucy's direction. Bits of meat and tomato flew off the ends of the spoon and splashed across Aunt Lucy's face, who scraped some off with her finger and promptly licked it off.

"Yum, I love Bolognese. The fresh basil you add really makes the sauce. Anyway, I was absolutely going to hex her."

"Kyran was here looking for you," Leanne said. "Apparently, you weren't subtle enough yesterday when going to find Eliza."

"When has Aunt Lucy ever been subtle?" Kaillie moaned.

"He'll get over it; he always does," Aunt Lucy said with a wave of her hand as Aunt Debbie took out her wand and muttered a spell. The pot of pasta on the stove flew to the sink and poured itself into a waiting colander while the pan full of Bolognese sauce carefully poured itself into a serving bowl before flying over to the dining table.

I watched in awe as Aunt Debbie continued to cast spells. Dishes and cutlery flew from the cupboards that opened without human help and soared toward the table, landing in a formation that would have made Martha Stewart proud.

"Will I learn how to do that?" I asked when Debbie finished and invited everyone over to the table.

"You will," she confirmed. "We're going to have to figure out exactly how to teach you the basics of magic."

"I'll do it," Aunt Lucy volunteered immediately.

"I'm not sure that's the best idea I've ever heard," Aunt Debbie said carefully as I sat down to eat. Dinner looked amazing. Kaillie handed me the bowl of spaghetti and I scooped up a pile and plopped it onto my plate, topping it with the Bolognese. I dug into the food as I listened to the others discuss the future of my magical education.

"Why not?" Aunt Lucy complained. "After all, I've got plenty of time on my hands, and I taught your daughter plenty of spells."

"Which I swear I never use," Kaillie said, her face paling.

"If it helps, I tried to convince Kaillie to use the spell that would turn someone's face into a watermelon when Mr. Johnson failed her on a science test back in ninth grade, but she refused," Leanne said.

"That's right, I did refuse!" Kaillie replied.

"See, this is why I don't want you teaching Eliza magic," Aunt Debbie said to her sister. "She needs to learn how to do simple things like making objects fly, and transforming *inanimate* objects into other things. She also needs to learn the basics of concoctology. She doesn't need you teaching her how to hex things. Or people. Especially people."

"I'll teach her magic that comes in handy in day-to-day life," Aunt Lucy retorted. "No one ever needed to know how to make a potion that makes your plants grow bigger. That's just not necessary in day-to-day life."

"Unless I decide I want to win the contest for the biggest zucchini at the state fair one year," I said with a grin.

"Now that gives me an idea…" Aunt Lucy said, trailing off.

"Absolutely not," Aunt Debbie said, her eyes flashing toward her sister.

"You never let me have any fun."

"You can have plenty of fun, so long as it doesn't involve using magic to get the best of the regular humans. Anyway, I think I'll take care of Eliza's magical education. As long as you're ok with that, of course," Aunt Debbie said, turning toward me.

I quickly swallowed the giant mouthful of spaghetti that was in my mouth before answering. "Yeah, that would be great."

"Perfect. We'll start tomorrow, after work. After all, I don't want to lose any time. You've got almost a quarter-century worth of learning to catch up on."

"I still think I'd be a much better teacher," Aunt Lucy said. "Now, I heard that for all the complaining you do about my way of life, you all managed to get one of your customers murdered at the coffee shop today."

"Well, it obviously wasn't any of us," Leanne replied. "I heard Dorothy was right, and Leonard was murdered."

Aunt Debbie nodded. "Yes. The medical examiner said he won't know for sure until he gets the results back from the toxicology test, but that he suspects it was poison. It's really quite disappointing; I'm worried word is going to get around town that people die from drinking our coffee."

"I'm worried that word is going to get back to the paranormal world that we did all of this," Kaillie muttered.

"Well, if he really was poisoned by our coffee, that means there can't have been all that many people who had access to him," Leanne pointed out. "I mean, there were us, and what, five customers in the café at the time? It had to be one of them who did it."

"You're right," I said breathlessly. "There weren't that many people there. And I don't think all of them even interacted with Leonard."

"Who *was* there?" Aunt Lucy asked, leaning forward in her seat expectantly.

"Well, there was Nancy Gerard," I said. "She was the one who tried to save Leonard's life."

"That's right," Leanne said. "I don't think she interacted with him at all until after he began to choke, so she couldn't have done it. Neither did Joe

Cleeves, but if anyone had a reason to kill Leonard it was him."

"Who's Joe Cleeves?" I asked.

"He was the man with the beer belly you served about five minutes before Leonard came in. Large cappuccino with extra froth. He's a property developer who owns a parcel of land next to the property Leonard and Roman live in. He's been trying to buy it off them, since it borders the water and he wants to build some condos or something on it. By all accounts, Roman was fine with them selling him the land, and really needed the money, but Leonard absolutely didn't want to."

"So you think Joe might have killed Leonard over the plot of land?" Kaillie asked, her mouth dropping open. "Surely not. Would he really kill someone over money?"

Leanne shrugged. "People have been killed for less."

"Yeah, but not on the island," Kaillie replied.

"Are you really so naïve that you think the greed of human nature doesn't exist on our little patch of paradise?" Aunt Lucy said. "I could absolutely see Joe killing Leonard to get a hold of that land. He could make millions selling condos there."

"There's only one problem," Leanne chimed in. "Joe was in the coffee shop, but he was sitting at the table furthest from Leonard, and he didn't leave his seat once. He was working on his computer the entire time. He couldn't have done it."

I nodded. I knew who Joe was now, and as far as I knew, Leanne was right. I hadn't seen him get up from his computer even once before Leonard's attack had begun.

"I can't believe this is a conversation we're having at dinner," Aunt Debbie said, shaking her head.

"Hey, it's the first time in years someone has been murdered here, and it was in the café our family owns. You have to let us speculate," Aunt Lucy retorted. "Who else was there?"

"Well, there was Dianne Mulgrew," Lucy said.

"Oh, she introduced herself to me," I said. "She works at the bank, as a teller, right?"

"That's her," Leanne confirmed.

"She seemed really nice. She went and spoke with Leonard at one point, right?"

"Yes," Leanne said. "I saw that as well. But then, what reason could she possibly have to want Leonard dead? Diane works at the bank, same as he does, but she's there during the day and he's there at night. It's not like they would have interacted much."

I nodded, and made a mental note to try and learn more about Dianne Mulgrew. After all, she had the opportunity to kill Leonard. Maybe she had done it.

"Don Kilmer also had the chance to kill him," Leanne said. "He walked past the table where Leonard had been sitting while Leonard was in the bathroom. He would have had to have been quick, but he could have slipped something into the mug without anyone noticing."

"Which one was Don?" I asked.

"The one who ordered two large coffees and drank them himself," Leanne asked. "How the guy doesn't die of a caffeine overdose I have no idea."

I laughed. "That's right, I remember him. He dropped a couple quarters into the tip jar on his way past Leonard's table and his hands were trembling."

"He's a good guy," Kaillie said. "He owns the hardware store here in town."

"I can't think of any reason he'd have to kill Leonard," Lucy mused. "Frankly, I'm surprised that brother of his didn't finally take him out."

"Roman?" I asked, and Lucy nodded.

"Yes. The fact that those two still lived under the same roof astounds me. They've been at each other's throats since their mother died."

"Oh?" Kaillie asked. "I knew they didn't get along, but I didn't realize it was so bad."

"It really was," Aunt Lucy said with a solemn nod. "You were only a child, so we kept a lot of the worst of it from you, but it was *bad*. At one point, the two of them got into a fistfight in the middle of Main Street. On a weekend in August. I've heard of deer coming out of the forest and causing traffic jams, but that was the first and last time I've seen one caused by two grown men going to town on one another."

"They were fighting over their mom's wishes, right?" Aunt Debbie asked.

"That's correct," Aunt Lucy replied. "The will said that old Roseanne Steele wanted to be cremated, and have her ashes scattered into the Pacific Ocean. But Roman insisted that in the day before she died Roseanne told him privately that she had changed her mind and wanted to be buried in the churchyard along with the rest of her family. There were no witnesses to this statement, so obviously it couldn't be considered, and Roseanne was cremated, her ashes scattered as per the written will. Roman never forgave Leonard for doing that to their mother, and they fought horribly for years since. I can't imagine what must have gone down under that roof without us knowing."

"There was that one time Roman went around with a black eye for a few weeks," Kaillie said. "I remember thinking he looked even scarier than usual when he walked past me down the street."

"Yes, that was about three months later," Aunt Lucy said, nodding. "We all knew Leonard had done it to him. The rumor at the time was that he hit him in the face with a frying pan. Some of us were taking bets as to how long it was going to be before one of them moved out."

"You say that as if it wasn't you running the pool," Aunt Debbie said pointedly to her sister. "And don't think I don't remember that you kept everyone's money."

Aunt Lucy shrugged. "As far as I'm concerned, the pool is still going. Besides, my money was on one of them murdering the other."

"Well, you lost," Leanne said with a grin. "Roman wasn't in the coffee shop that day."

"In that case, everyone lost, and as the pool organizer, I get to keep the money," Aunt Lucy announced. "No harm no foul."

"I'm pretty sure that's not how it's supposed to work," Kaillie said with a small smile.

"Yeah, well, half the people who initially placed bets are dead now anyway," Aunt Lucy said with a shrug. "And I'm sure the rest have forgotten."

"There was one other person I saw speaking with Leonard," I interrupted, wanting to get the conversation back onto the murder. After all, if I was going to try and find out who killed him, I needed to know who my suspects were. "Another man, older, grey hair. Very thin, ordered a coffee and a muffin."

"Oh, Jack," Leanne said, nodding. "Jack Frost. And yes, that is his real name. He's a retired math teacher."

"He was one of my favorite teachers," Kaillie said with a fond smile. "He was always willing to stay late and explain a concept you didn't understand."

"Yeah, he's good people," Leanne confirmed. "Although I do wish he had bumped my C+ up to a B back in tenth grade."

"Would he have had any reason to kill Leonard?" I

asked, and all the other heads around the table shook in unison.

"Nope. Jack's a good man. You'll get to know him better soon; he comes in at least a couple of times a week."

Aunt Lucy gave me a curious look, but I carefully ignored it and slurped up another mouthful of spaghetti. There were three people who could have murdered Leonard Steele. Now I just had to figure out which one of them actually did it.

CHAPTER 12

The following day I went back to the coffee shop with Aunt Debbie, who got the call just after four in the morning that the crime scene technicians had finished and we were welcome to open up again. I was a little bit worried about what peoples' reactions were going to be. What if everyone felt the same way as Ariadne Stewart? What if people saw I was the one taking orders and immediately left, thinking I was going to poison them? What if I really wasn't welcome in this town anymore?

I tried not to think too hard about these things, but it was hard to do so when the first customer of the day walked up to the door, had their hand on the handle, made eye contact with me behind the counter and immediately turned around and walked the other way instead.

"Oh, I've got to get out of here," I said to Leanne.

"I'm hurting business already."

"Nonsense," Leanne said, taking my hand and giving it a quick squeeze. "So there's an idiot or two out there who thinks badly of you. So what? You're a part of this family now, and that means sticking up for one another. We're not going to just throw you in the back and hide you away just because a few people in town don't like you."

"Thanks," I said, managing a small smile. I did like the fact that she was sticking up for me; apart from Dad I had never really had that in my life before.

"Even if people think you did it, don't worry. They'll move on. In a week or two everything will have been forgotten, and they'll go back to normal. You never know; the cops might even figure out who killed Leonard Steele."

"You say that like it's not a foregone conclusion," I said with a laugh.

"That's because you haven't met our police chief, Ronald Jones," Leanne said. "He makes the navigator of the Hindenburg look like an aerial ace."

"That much of a train wreck, huh?"

"He's old as dirt, an alcoholic, and once famously caught a couple of tourists transacting a drug deal underneath the window outside his office. He told them to keep it down and slammed the window shut. One of the other officers heard the commotion, wondered what was going on in the alley outside the police station and found the culprits."

"Wow," I said, giggling. "How does the guy still manage to have a job?"

Leanne shrugged. "The fact that this isn't exactly a high-crime area, I guess. There hasn't been a murder in years, burglaries are virtually unheard of, and petty crime is basically the only thing that happens here. It's not a great idea to commit a crime on an island where the only way out is via a ferry that runs a couple times a day."

"Fair enough, but shouldn't he still have been ousted years ago?"

"Probably, but he's never screwed anything up badly enough to get fired, or have it suggested that he retire," Leanne said with a shrug. "The drug thing was bad, but they managed to sweep it under the carpet in their report, so the higher-ups that make these decisions never found out about it."

"So there's basically no chance that the person who actually killed Leonard is going to get caught," I said, frowning. "That sucks. That means everyone is going to think I did it."

Leanne gave me a sympathetic look. "It will go away. I promise. This is a good place, and most of the people who live here are reasonable. I know it sucks, but people will start coming back."

I nodded, distracted by the entrance of Janice, who flashed me a huge smile as soon as she saw me. "Eliza! So nice to see you again."

"Thank you, same to you," I said, giving her a warm

smile. Maybe Leanne was right: not everyone was going to automatically assume I was a killer.

"It's such a shame what happened to Leonard yesterday. I've heard he was murdered. Can you imagine? Who would do such a thing?" Janice shook her head sadly.

"I don't know, but I hope the killer is found," I said.

"I hope you're right," Janice said. "It terrifies me to think someone willing to go to those lengths is living among us here on the island. Of course, I'd feel quite a bit better about things if we had stronger leadership in the police force, but at least a few of the detectives the chief has working for him aren't idiots. Hopefully they figure it out."

"I think they will," Leanne said. "This is a small town, and there weren't that many people who had the opportunity to kill him."

"Yes. I'll put it out to the universe that the killer be found, and hopefully the cosmos will answer."

Janice placed her order once more, which Leanne had already been making for her, thanked us, and left.

"See? That wasn't so bad," Leanne said to me. "Don't let the people who don't know you get you down. They'll come around."

I really hoped Leanne was right.

For the next few hours I continued to take orders. We began to get enough customers that I no longer had time to worry whether or not any of them thought I was a murderer, and I made sure that when I poured the brewed coffee into cups from the large containers I did it from the side so that the customers could see I wasn't slipping poison into their drinks.

During a quiet period, a familiar-looking woman walked in. I recognized her; it was Dianne Mulgrew, the woman who had stopped and had a chat with Leonard while he was drinking his coffee.

"Hello, welcome to Cackling Witch Coffee," I said to her. "What can I get for you today?"

"A twelve ounce latte and a blueberry muffin, please," she said to me, handing over a bill. Her eyes darted over to the table where Leonard had been sitting the day before, where he had died.

"It's such a tragedy, isn't it?" I offered in a quiet voice.

"It truly is. I was speaking to him just a couple of minutes before it happened." Dianne shook her head.

"What were you speaking with him about? You two worked together, right?"

"Well, we both worked at the bank, that much is true. But we didn't work *together*. He was the security guard, so his shift started right as mine ended at the end of the day. I knew he was seeing the doctor about his heart, and I hadn't seen him since, so I was just asking how he was doing."

"Oh, I didn't know that," I said. "I didn't know him at all; yesterday when I served him was the first time that I met him."

There was a slightly awkward pause for a moment.

"Of course, right. Well, he told me he was diagnosed with high blood pressure. Frankly, I was surprised he wasn't diagnosed earlier, given how cantankerous he could be. He even showed me the pills he had to take and complained about the doctors making him take them." Dianne smiled sadly. "I mentioned to him that they were obviously good for his health, and Leonard complained that his bad ticker came from his father's side of the family, but that he wasn't going to let genetics get the best of him. Then he swallowed one of the capsules whole and said the pharmaceutical industry could go to hell, and that for what that pill cost, it should taste like maple syrup. That was Leonard. It's sad to think that was the last conversation I'd ever have with him."

"It sounds like you were fond of him. Not a lot of people in this town were, from what I've heard."

"Oh, I was. Leonard was a grouch, no doubt about that. There was a reason he worked at night, when he didn't have to interact with other people. And the whole situation with his brother was awful. But he wasn't a bad person, deep down, so I always tried to be nice to him. You never know what someone else is going through, after all."

"My dad always said that," I said softly, finding the tears coming to my eyes yet again. I still cried so easily at the thought of him. I blinked back the tears and took a deep breath to steady myself.

"He sounds like a smart man," Dianne said. "That's

why I was always nice to Leonard. As far as I knew, he never did anything really bad to anybody, and he didn't deserve what happened to him."

"Well, hopefully the police will find out who did this."

"I certainly hope so," Dianne said as Leanne brought her coffee over to her. "He may not have been the easiest person to get along with, but as far as I know, he never did anything to deserve to be murdered."

Obviously, someone disagreed. It could have been Dianne, but after speaking with her I didn't think she was the person I should be focusing on. She seemed like a genuinely nice human being who reached out to Leonard when not a lot of people would.

A moment later, the door opened once more, and when I looked at the person who walked in my breath caught in my throat. It was Leonard!

No, on second thought, it wasn't him. But my goodness was there a family resemblance. Their faces were exactly the same shape, but this man had a slightly larger nose, and his eyes were rounder, and more deep-set. Apart from that, the two men could have been identical.

He confirmed my suspicions as soon as he made his way to the counter and spoke.

"Everyone is saying this is the coffee shop where my brother died. Is that true?"

So this was Roman. "It is. I'm sorry for your loss," I replied.

"Well, I'm not. As far as I'm concerned, Leonard should have left this earth years ago. I'm not sad he's dead. My only hope is that the medical examiner treats his body the way Leonard would have hated, the way he forced us to do with my mother."

Wow. Roman Steele was not mincing words. I had no idea what to reply, so I kind of just gaped at the man. That didn't seem to bother him; he just kept talking.

"So it was here that he died. Good. He had it coming, quite frankly. I still can't believe he did our mother that way. She *told* me what she wanted. Told me just a few hours before she died. And all because Leo wouldn't believe me when I told him we had to go through all that trouble, just to have mom buried in the churchyard. She wouldn't have wanted that, you know. She didn't want that. Didn't want it at all, but he made her get cremated all the same. She should have been buried, her body with her family. That was what she really wanted. She loved her family, mom did. But now he's dead, and I'm glad for it."

"Do you want a coffee or anything?" I finally managed to stammer out, not exactly knowing where this insane rant was going.

"Eh?" Roman asked, surprised, as if he didn't realize where he was. "Oh, a coffee? Nah. I just came here to see the spot where that no-good brother of mine finally died. I'll do everything I can to make sure he isn't buried next to mom. He doesn't deserve to spend eternity next to such a good woman."

And with that, Roman rapped his knuckles on the counter a couple of times, looked around, nodded as if satisfied with what he saw, and walked back out.

I widened my eyes at Leanne, who wiggled her eyebrows at me.

"I told you he was a little bit strange. They both were."

"You were not kidding," I replied. "But hey, grief makes people act in strange ways."

"I don't know, that didn't seem to me like a man who was grieving his brother."

I shrugged. "I barely remember what I did the first few days after Dad died. Grief does weird things to you. Roman might make some decisions now, do some things and say some things he'll regret later."

"Maybe," Leanne said, but she didn't seem convinced.

Either way, I wasn't going to judge Roman too harshly. There was absolutely no way he was the killer – I would have noticed him being in the coffee shop at the same time as his brother – which meant he couldn't have killed him. So he had just lost his brother. The two might have hated each other, but I figured when you lived under the same roof as someone for what was probably sixty-some years, losing them suddenly like that would have an effect, regardless of how well you got along.

CHAPTER 13

The rest of the morning passed by without incident, to my immense relief. A part of me was genuinely worried that Cackling Witch Coffee was going to spontaneously explode, or something along those lines, given how my last few attempts at making it through a whole day of work without disaster had gone.

I was worried that we would have fewer customers, but in fact, the opposite happened. I got asked so many times what table Leonard was sitting at when he died from wide-eyed lookie-loos that it appeared the risk of being poisoned to death while eating here wasn't so strong that it kept people from coming in to see the spot for themselves.

It made me feel pretty icky, personally. A man had *died*. Sure, he wasn't a very well-liked man, and it appeared no one in town was really going to miss him all that much – Dianne was the first person who had even attempted to make him out to be human – but that didn't make it any less weird to have people coming by to stare, as far as I was concerned.

A few minutes before my lunch break was set to begin, Jack Frost – I giggled inwardly at the name – walked through the door and made his way toward me.

"Hello," I greeted him warmly. "What can I get for you?"

"A regular coffee and a chocolate chip banana muffin, please," he asked, pulling out some pre-counted change and handing it over to me. This was obviously his regular order; it was also what he had asked for the day before.

"You used to be a teacher, right?" I asked, and Jack smiled.

"Yes, that was me. Leanne here was one of my students in the last year before I retired."

Leanne flashed him a smile and a wave. "You were one of the best, Mr. Frost."

"Please, you know you should just call me Jack now."

"Sorry, you'll always be Mr. Frost to me."

"Ah well, you win some, you lose some," Jack said to me with a hearty laugh. "You're new to town, aren't you?"

"I am," I explained. "I'm Leanne's cousin. My mom, Patricia, was Leanne's mom's sister."

"Oh, you're Patricia and Daniel's little girl. Why, I

actually remember when you were born. Both your parents were in my classes. They pretended to hate each other at the time, but I had a sneaking suspicion they were going to end up together. I took great pleasure in being right. Of course, it was a tragedy what happened to your mother."

I nodded sadly as Jack continued. "So what brings you back to town now? Is your father still in town? Last I heard he had moved, and taken you with him after Patricia died, but none of us ever found out where."

"San Francisco," I said. "That was where I grew up. Unfortunately, dad died a few months ago."

"Oh, I'm so sorry. Your father was a good man."

"He was," I agreed. "What was he like as a teenager, if I may ask?"

"Of course. I very much enjoy reminiscing on my old students. He was a rambunctious young man. He played football, and he was quite good at it, if I remember correctly. He was the kind of person who was always on the go, never sitting still. Even in class he would always have one leg jiggling, like he couldn't bear to sit still for even a single second."

I smiled. That certainly did sound like Dad. He played soccer with a bunch of his coworkers every Tuesday night after I was old enough to be left alone at the apartment for a few hours.

"And my mom?"

"Well, she was almost the opposite. Patricia was

quite quiet, and thoughtful. She would always think before she spoke, and I never heard her say a mean thing about anybody. She studied very hard, and got excellent grades. I wasn't the least bit surprised when she graduated and went to Washington State. Daniel went there as well; he was a Husky. We were all very proud of them. They didn't run in the same circles at all, but I think having someone from home that they could talk to was good for the both of them. That was where they eventually fell in love. I don't think anyone saw it coming; they were so different. But Patricia was good for Daniel. She taught him to think a little bit before he spoke, and he taught her to get out of her comfort zone a little bit. After they graduated they both came back to the island, and a few years later you were born."

"Wow," I said, emotions getting the better of me. "I didn't know any of that. Thank you."

"Did your father not talk about his past?"

I shook my head. "He didn't talk about my mom at all. I knew almost nothing about her. I know he missed her terribly; when I was young I caught him crying a couple of times when he didn't think I was around."

"Oh, yes," Jack said, nodding solemnly. "Daniel loved Patricia. That much was obvious to anybody who saw the two of them together."

"Why didn't he tell me about her, though?" I asked, not expecting a real answer. It was something that had bothered me ever since I found out about this side of the family. Dad had never told me about any of them. Why had he hidden it?

"We all have our reasons," Jack said with a shrug. "Perhaps he simply found it too painful to talk about."

I nodded, then remembered that I wasn't supposed to talk about my parents with Jack, but rather figure out if he was the person who had murdered Leonard.

"You were here yesterday, weren't you?" I asked, and Jack nodded.

"When Leonard passed on? Yes, I was. That poor man." Jack shook his head sadly. "I spoke with him only a couple of moments before it happened."

"Oh?"

"Yes, he was trying to get me to help him with a legal problem he was having with his brother. Roman wanted to sell the property they were living on, and Leonard didn't. He wanted me to help him show to his brother that they were financially better off by hanging onto the land, or selling it to someone else. I believe he was going to try and argue that ideally they would continue to live on the property for the next ten years or so."

"And did you help him?"

Jack shrugged. "I told him there was nothing I could do. After all, it was a family matter, and I'm not an expert in real estate transactions. I could teach him how to do trigonometry, but predicting the future of the real estate market was not in my skillset. I told him he needed to speak with a real estate professional."

"How did he react to that?"

Jack shrugged. "He seemed angry, but that was par for the course for Leonard. He was muttering about Roman ruining everything, and how first he had tried to destroy their mother's memory, and now this. There was a lot of animosity between those two, and there had been for years. It was quite sad to see, really."

"Wow," I said.

"Yes, I think Roman will be very happy that his brother is gone, and that's a tragedy. If you ask me, they never should have been living under the same roof, but they were both too stubborn to leave."

"It sounds like it was a sad situation all around," I said, grabbing the muffin from the display case and putting it on a plate for Jack.

"Oh, it really was. The fights between those two men were legendary here in town. I'm sure their mother would have been incredibly disappointed to see what became of them both. She would have wanted them to get along, but not even her memory could do that. After Roman claimed that she had changed her wishes, and then been denied, there was no chance of reconciliation between the two. Frankly, I'm surprised. If anyone was going to kill Leonard, I would have thought it was Roman."

I nodded slowly. "Right. But no, that's impossible."

"It is, and yet I can't think of who else could have wanted Leonard dead. I supposed there was a lot of money in that deal he was refusing to let through. People have been killed for less."

I poured the coffee and passed it to Jack. "That is true." Jack thanked me and headed to a table at the back, and I pursed my lips, thinking hard about his words.

I didn't think he was the killer either. Maybe I was just too optimistic to be a proper detective. I automatically assumed the best of everyone, but Jack had seemed like a genuinely friendly and nice guy. And I appreciated that he told me about my parents.

If I was lucky, Don Kilmer would come in soon wearing a t-shirt saying 'I did it', but I couldn't exactly count on that.

CHAPTER 14

When we finally closed up shop at the end of the day I breathed a sigh of relief. I had finally gotten through a full day of work without a major disaster. No one died. I didn't fly through a mall on a broom. As far as I was concerned, I considered it to be a massive success.

Leanne and Aunt Debbie showed me how to clean up for the night, and we packed up the leftover baked goods to sell for cheap the following day. I got a ride home with Aunt Debbie, and when she pulled into the driveway she killed the engine and turned toward me.

"I think we should do your first magic lesson before dinner. How does that sound?"

Frankly, it sounded terrifying. I was still coming to grips with the idea that magic still existed, and there was a part of me that wasn't one hundred percent convinced that I actually had magical powers. What if I was the exception? What if I was like Leanne, who hadn't inherited them? I knew I had flown around on that broom, but what if there was a different explanation for that?

"Sure," were the words that came out of my mouth, though. "That sounds great."

It didn't sound great at all.

I followed Debbie into the main living room, where she went to a cabinet and pulled out a wand. It was a plain piece of wood, a little under a foot long, painted a nice shade of pastel purple.

"I hope you're ok with this wand," Aunt Debbie said, handing it to me. "We don't have a ton of options out here I'm afraid. If you have specific requirements you could always ask Kyran if he would buy you one. Wands are only available to buy in the paranormal world, and of course, we don't have access to that."

"This is fine, it's actually quite pretty," I said, taking the wand carefully from Aunt Debbie. A part of me wanted to wave it around and pretend I was Hermione Granger, but another part of me was overly cautious about doing anything with it at all. After all, I didn't want to accidentally set a couch on fire or anything like that.

"Feel free to just hold it normally," Aunt Debbie said with a kind smile, obviously noticing my hesitation. "You're not going to do anything by accident. I promise. You have to cast an incantation before anything will happen when you hold the wand."

"Ok," I said, gripping the wood with more confidence that I wasn't going to mess anything up completely. "So there are chants you have to say to perform magic?"

"That's right," Aunt Debbie said, rifling around a cabinet and pulling out a notebook and a pen. "I'll make you a list of all the spells I teach you, and that way you can memorize them on your own time. Now, every coven has their own spells. We're members of the coven of Saturn, which is an air coven. We're witches who are naturally more skilled at everything that involves air – for example, dealing with the weather, or riding a broom."

I barked out a laugh at that last comment. "I guess I'm the exception that proves the rule."

Aunt Debbie gave me a kind smile. "Don't write yourself off just yet. You had absolutely no idea what you were doing; you didn't even know magic existed. You can't be expected to be perfect at everything straight away. But you may find that you take to broom riding faster than witches from other covens. If we knew any of them, anyway. Besides, you don't need to start riding a broom anytime soon."

"But we can change the weather?" I asked. "Does that mean we can single-handedly take care of climate change?"

Aunt Debbie laughed gently. "Unfortunately, no.

Every witch has a certain amount of magical energy inside of her. Whenever you cast a spell, some of that energy is used up. It regenerates automatically through rest and through not using magic, but it means that there are limits on how much magic you can use before your energy stores are depleted and your magic no longer works."

"Ok, so basically you're saying that it would take way too much energy to change the weather in the entire world all the time?"

"That's right. So while you could cast a spell to make it rain on Enchanted Enclave for a small period of time you wouldn't be able to turn this place into a tropical island. And frankly, that's probably for the best. Nature is supposed to stay wild, unaffected by our magic."

I nodded in understanding. "Alright, that makes sense."

"So, the most basic spells are those in which you transform ordinary, inanimate objects. Changing their size and color are the most common ways to start learning spells, so I'm going to teach you those ones first."

I gripped the wand harder in my hand. "Ok."

"Now, I'll show you how it's done first. You cast the incantation, and as you're saying the words, you need to imagine the change happening to the item you're casting the spell toward. The better you can imagine the change in your head, the better the spell is going to go."

"Got it," I said.

"Alright," Aunt Debbie said. She grabbed a candle off the bookshelf. It was plain white, and she placed it in the middle of the coffee table, motioning for me to take a seat on the couch in front of it, which I did.

"Now, we're going to change the color of this candle to start with. Repeat after me: *Saturn, god of plenty, in this world there are colors many. Turn this candle blue.*"

I gasped as the candle in front of me instantly changed into a deep blue. "Wow."

"Now it's your turn," Aunt Debbie said to me. "Don't get discouraged if it doesn't work at first. Do you remember the words I used?"

I nodded. Taking a deep breath, I gripped the wand and pointed it at the candle, doing the best I could to imagine it going from the color of the deep ocean to a shade of canary. "*Saturn, god of plenty, in this world there are colors many. Turn this candle yellow.*"

I let out a squeal of surprise as sure enough, the candle immediately turned a vivid yellow.

"You did it!" Aunt Debbie said, clapping her hands together with delight. "Good job!"

I couldn't stop staring at the candle. This was it. I had done it. I had actually used magic. All of this was real. It wasn't some insane, elaborate prank. I was really a witch, and I had just magically changed the color of a candle.

This whole situation was going from 'terrifying' to 'pretty darn cool' very quickly.

"Now, I want you to try it again," Aunt Debbie said. "I know it's a simple spell, but the more you practice, the better you're going to get."

I nodded and focused once more. This time, I changed the candle from yellow to green. I then cast the spell again and went from green to red. The more I cast the spell, the more I felt like I had just gone for a long run. After the fourth time I cast the spell, I was definitely starting to feel tired.

"Alright, that's enough," Aunt Debbie said to me with a smile. "You're obviously getting tired."

"Is that how quickly magical energy runs out?" I asked. "But you send all the food and dishes flying over to the dinner table and it looks like it doesn't take anything out of you."

"Your magical powers are like a muscle. It's going to take time for them to grow. I've been using my magic for decades now, whereas this is your first time. Keep practicing, and you're going to get there. I promise."

"Ok," I said, handing Aunt Debbie the wand, but she took my hand and pushed it gently back toward me.

"This is yours now. You need to hang onto it. You might only know this one spell, but practice it. Whenever you're alone, or around family, feel free to practice this spell on whatever tickles your fancy. The more you work at it, the better you're going to get. And tomorrow I'll show you another spell. Slowly but surely you'll catch up, and you'll be using magic like it's second nature to you in no time. Now, if you'll excuse me, it's taco night, and I need to get everything ready."

"Thanks for the lesson," I said, waving my wand around aimlessly, pretending to do magic. I had literally just changed the color of a candle! That was pretty awesome.

CHAPTER 15

As it turned out, taco Sunday took place as a celebration for making it through another work week, as Cackling Witch Coffee was closed on Mondays and Tuesdays.

I woke up late the next morning, lazed around in bed for a few extra minutes while enjoying the beauty of not having to be at work at six in the morning, and eventually managed to drag myself out of bed to the kitchen.

I was pleasantly surprised to see a giant stack of pancakes waiting for me, complete with fresh berries, syrup and whipped cream to pour on top.

"Wow, this looks amazing," I said to Aunt Debbie, who was still standing in front of the stove.

"Help yourself," she said, motioning to everything. "I'm going to go into town later if you'd like a ride. Or, if you'd like, you can see where your cousins live if you'd prefer to live with them. Don't worry, I won't be insulted if you do. You are welcome to stay here for as long as you'd like, of course."

"Thank you," I said warmly as I grabbed three pancakes and doused them in syrup. "I really appreciate how nice you've all been to me."

"That's what family is for. Now, why don't you finish those off, and before you get going we can do a quick magic lesson? I was thinking I might show you how to change the size of that candle today."

"Great," I said as I made my way to the breakfast bar. "I'm looking forward to that." My attitude toward magical lessons had changed since yesterday. Rather than dreading it, I was starting to finally embrace this new side of my life.

Two hours later I was feeling drained once more, and decided to go into town to explore. I wanted to stop by the hardware store and see if I could have a chat with Don Kilmer, who had walked past Leonard's table when it was empty. Frankly, I figured he had the best opportunity to poison Leonard, since all he would have had to do was slip the poison into the coffee. Leonard wouldn't have been able to see it happen.

I was ecstatic about my improvements on the magical front. I had managed to make the candle bigger *and* smaller, and I was looking forward to getting to practice my magic further later on in the day. I started keeping my wand inside my purse at all times, since, as Aunt Debbie reminded me, a witch had to be ready one hundred percent of the time. You never knew when you were going to need to use magic.

Aunt Debbie drove me into town. "Where would you like to be dropped off?" she asked kindly.

"Oh, just on Main Street," I replied. "Can you point out the hardware store for me?"

Aunt Debbie gave me a curious look, but did as I asked. She pointed out a low brick building, painted blue, with "Kilmer Hardware" printed on an old, faded wooden sign.

"That's the place," she said. "Don is a nice guy. He'll help you find anything you need."

"Thanks," I said with a smile, jumping out. "Don't worry about giving me a ride back home. I'll find my way."

Aunt Debbie nodded at me with a smile as I jumped out of the car and made my way to the store. It was a gorgeous spring morning; a little bit on the colder side for me, being used to San Francisco weather, but the sun shone high in the sky and the first birds of the season – or perhaps a few that didn't fly south for the winter in the first place - flew between the trees on either side of the road, chirping away.

I stepped into the store and an old-fashioned bell above me rang out, announcing my entrance. This was everything I had expected a small-town hardware store to look like: shelves packed tightly together, every single inch of available space from floor to ceiling displaying something that local homeowners might need but didn't want to go to the mainland to retrieve. To my right was a single counter, with the man I was looking for organizing a display of batteries next to it. He turned when he heard the bell.

"Hi there," he said. "You're the new girl who works at the coffee shop, aren't you?"

"That's me," I said with a smile. "I'm Eliza."

"Don," he replied, holding out a hand, which I shook. "Nice to meet you. I hear you're Daniel Emory's daughter."

"Correct," I said. "Listen, I was wondering if you could tell me about Leonard, the man who died in the coffee shop the other day. I was told you knew him."

Don nodded. "I did, yeah. For a man who hated people so much, he sure knew a lot of them."

"So you agree with the others that he wasn't a very nice man?"

"Oh, he definitely wasn't," Don said with a dry laugh. "The man was hellish to deal with. His brother too, but at least his brother was on the right side of things."

"The right side of things?" I asked.

"There's a developer in town who's looking to buy the empty parcel of land adjacent to the property Leonard and his brother live on. The brothers own the land; it used to belong to their mother."

"Joe Cleeves? I heard about him."

"That's the one. He wants to build waterfront condos on the land, which is a fantastic idea. They'll bring a handful more visitors to the island, who will go ahead and spend their money here, and the spot is beautiful. It's right on the Pacific Ocean. Roman, the sensible of the two brothers, was all for it. As far as he was concerned that piece of land was useless, and with land prices the way they are on the island, he was absolutely willing to sell. But Leonard didn't want to. He said there was a pod of sea lions that used that part of the beach as their home, and he was worried that they would be driven off."

"So his objection was all about land use?"

"That's right," Don said. "As far as I could tell, anyway. Last time I spoke with Joe he was quite annoyed about it. He kept telling me how Leonard was just being an old hippie, and how times had changed, and the sea lions would find somewhere else to live."

"Do you think the project will go through now?"

"I don't see why not," Don replied with a shrug. "It might take some time, since the estate will have to officially pass to Roman, but after it's his free and clear, I'm sure he's going to sell it on to Joe like he'd planned."

"Do you know Joe well?"

"Sure," Don nodded. "I consider him a friend. He's a good guy. Because of what he does he's in here quite a bit, so I see him on a weekly basis."

"Alright, thanks," I said.

"No problem. Anything I can help you find?"

"No, I just wanted to find out some more about Leonard."

"Fair enough. I imagine it must have been quite a shock for you, getting to town and having Leonard die on your first day at work."

"It was," I admitted. "A lot of people seem to think I'm the one who killed him."

Don shook his head. "That's ridiculous. If anyone in town had no reason to off the guy it was you. You didn't even know him, right?"

"Yeah."

"Well, hopefully Chief Ronald manages to get his head out of his butt for fifteen whole seconds and manages to solve this thing. I didn't like Leonard, and I thought he was on the wrong side of the deal with Joe, but there was no reason to kill the guy." Don shook his head. "I can't imagine who might have done it. I guess Roman is probably the only person I could see being angry enough to do it."

That seemed to be the consensus here in town.

"Alright, well, thanks for the help."

"No problem."

I made my way back out onto the street, thinking over what Don had told me. It hit me as I was walking that there was one person with a reason to want Leonard dead that I hadn't considered before: Don himself. After all, Joe was a customer of his, and if he worked as a property developer, I assumed a fairly big one. If Joe managed to buy the land and develop the property, I assumed he would be buying at least a few things from Don's hardware store. After all, the major stuff would almost certainly be ordered in bulk from the mainland and shipped in, but projects like that always had last-minute items that needed to be purchased, and it would be much easier for him to do it by buying from his local friend than going all the way back to the mainland.

Of course, Joe was the even better suspect. The project would be worth millions of dollars to him, potentially, whereas I assumed Don would only get a few grand in extra purchases, tops. I might have been wrong about that, though.

Then of course, Don mentioned that he and Joe were good friends. What if they were *really* good friends, and that Joe hired Don to kill Leonard? That was also a possibility.

As I made my way down the street, I was convinced: Don was at the top of my suspect list. He was the only one with the opportunity *and* reason to kill Leonard.

I was going to be focusing on him in the future.

CHAPTER 16

I decided I needed to go back and find some information about Don. After all, if he was the killer, I had to prove it. Maybe he still had some of the poison he had used to murder Leonard in the store. After all, that was probably where he had kept it.

Hardware stores were full of poisons. I didn't know what he had used, but it had to be incredibly fast-acting to have killed Leonard so quickly. The man must have only had a sip or two of the coffee after coming back from the bathroom before he was found dead. I assumed if he'd simply given Leonard one of the poisons commonly found in the shop, like rat poison, it would have taken quite a bit longer to take effect.

That meant I was looking for something different. Maybe something along the lines of some poisonous mushroom powder, or belladonna, or something. I didn't really know all that much about poisons, on the basis that I wasn't a complete and total psychopath. Basically everything I knew about poisoning people came from TV shows and movies.

But how on earth was I going to manage it? I needed to get back into the store without him seeing me, and somehow have a look around. It wasn't like Don was going to just let me peek through every little inch of his store.

That meant I was going to have to wait until the store was closed, and sneak around after dark, hoping that I didn't get caught. Great. I was going to have to commit one crime to prove that I didn't commit a second crime.

"Hey, Eliza," a voice called out from behind me, and I turned to see Leanne and Kaillie waving at me from up ahead. "What are you doing in town?"

"Oh, you know, just running through some errands," I answered, shrugging my shoulders nonchalantly. "And you guys?"

"I have to stop at the bank, and then we were going to get lunch," Kaillie answered. "Why don't you come with us? You still have to open a bank account here, right? I mean, I know you could keep your account from San Francisco, but First Enchanted Bank is the only branch in town, and it's going to be handy long-term if you at least open an account here."

"Yeah, ok," I said. "That's a good idea."

The three of us made our way to what was hands-down the biggest building on Main Street. Three stories high and built of brick, it looked like what I always imagined the old-school original buildings for banks back on the East Coast would have looked like. It was like stepping back into the 1800s as we walked into the building. A giant chandelier hung down from the ceiling, casting a warm light throughout the space. White and black tiles lined the floor that led to the wooden teller counters, which was where Leanne and Kaillie immediately walked, with me following after them.

Dianne Mulgrew noticed us then, her teller space open, and waved us over.

"Well if it isn't my three favorite cackling witches," she said with a wink as we walked to her station. "Though I don't get to see nearly enough of you, Kaillie, what with you always out the back baking."

"Well, I'm better at baking than making coffee," Kaillie laughed. "That's more Leanne's domain. I always end up burning the beans."

"Hey, if you keep making those blueberry scones, I'm not going to complain," Dianne replied. "What can I help you with today?"

"Well, I just need to get a money order for mom, but Eliza needs to open a new bank account."

"Oh, sure, I can do that for you," Dianne said. "Come on over here to one of the offices where we can sit down."

Dianne tapped away at the computer for a minute, presumably logging herself out, then motioned for us to follow her to a small, private room with a few chairs in front of a desk. "Alright, let's do the money order first," she said, and Leanne handed her over a slip of paper with the information she needed.

"I know you need your days off as well, but I must say, it makes Mondays that much worse when I don't get to have my coffee," Dianne said with a laugh.

"Well, you come in on the weekends, which are your days off, so that makes up for it," Leanne replied. "You should start drinking iced coffee, then you can just keep it in the fridge until the next day."

"Now there's an idea," Dianne said with a wink. "I'm just glad you weren't forced to close for longer than that afternoon. I was talking to my mother the other day and she said years ago, when there was a murder at the pool back in the seventies, they kept the place shut for a whole week. Right in the middle of summer, too."

Kaillie shuddered. "Who would possibly want to swim in a pool where they found a body, though?"

"Oh, the body wasn't actually *in* the pool. The woman had been killed in the showers. She'd had an argument with another woman about something, I can't remember the details anymore. But she was shoved, slipped over, and hit her head on the tiles on the way down. A big shame, but an accident. Not like this. I heard from Lucy's Floozies that he was killed with wolfsbane," Dianne said. "They were all in here earlier."

"Where did that name come from, anyway?" I asked.

"Aunt Lucy decided she wanted to reclaim it, and that there was nothing wrong with a woman deciding to be a floozy," Leanne replied. "You saw my mom?" she continued, looking at Dianne.

"Your mom is one of Lucy's Floozies?" I asked, and Leanne nodded.

"Yeah. It drives dad insane, since the two of them have been divorced for about five years. He doesn't understand how his ex-wife can be one of his sister's best friends, but there you have it."

I laughed. "That sounds about right. It must make Thanksgiving dinner fun."

"Oh, you can't even *imagine* Thanksgiving at Aunt Debbie's," Leanne said.

Dianne laughed. "Yes, your family isn't exactly known for being the most normal in town."

"Wait," Kaillie said. "Let's go back to the wolfsbane. Was that Dorothy who got that information?"

"Yes," Dianne said. "One of the detectives – I just can't imagine it having been Ron – told the medical examiner to put a rush on the toxicology results, and apparently that's what killed him."

"Ground wolfsbane," I repeated, my mind whirring with possibilities. That wasn't the sort of thing that was ordinarily sold at a hardware store, which meant if Don Kilmer hadn't gotten rid of it yet, it would have to be hidden somewhere. I still figured inside the store would be the most likely; he would have come from the store to the coffee shop, so presumably he kept the poison there rather than at his home.

"It creeps me out to think that happened here," Kaillie said. "And in our coffee shop."

"I agree," Dianne said. "Frankly, I'd be happier if they found who did it as soon as possible. I don't like knowing someone willing to do that is walking around town unchecked. After all, I have a daughter who lives here. I'd feel a lot better if I knew the murderer wasn't running free. I really do hope it's not someone from here. I don't like the idea that someone willing to do this has been here around us all this time." She looked at me, as if realizing what she'd said, and quickly stammered on. "Not you, of course, Eliza. You're obviously not the killer. You had no reason to want Leonard dead."

Presumably neither would anyone else who was new to town, I thought to myself, but I didn't reply. My heart sank as I was once again made aware of just how much of an outsider I was here, and how I knew that if the killer wasn't found, people would always be asking questions about how much of a coincidence it was that Leonard was killed immediately after I showed up.

I had to do whatever I could to clear my name and find the real killer.

CHAPTER 17

By the time we left the bank it was high time for lunch.

"Should we go to Otterly Delicious again?" I asked, earning a laugh from Leanne.

"Already an addict, are we? Well good, it means you're well and truly a local here now."

The three of us made our way to the diner. I settled on a BLT, fries and a lemonade today, and the three of us made our way toward the tables only to find Aunt Lucy already sitting at one of the booths at the far end.

"We heard you were at the bank this morning," Kaillie said, slipping into the booth next to her while Leanne and I took the other side.

"I was," Lucy replied. "We're looking into Dianne. She's one of the suspects in Leonard's murder, after all."

"You *cannot* mean you're trying to solve this," Kaillie said, her mouth dropping open.

"Why not?" Aunt Lucy said with a shrug. "This is the first interesting thing that's happened in this town in years. Besides, our police chief couldn't find his own butthole with both hands, so if someone else doesn't get involved there isn't a chance in the world that the killer's going to be found."

"So you obviously decided *you* were the perfect choice to play Batman and try and find the murderer yourself," Leanne said, crossing her arms in front of her.

"Obviously, except I'm way hotter than Christian Bale," Aunt Lucy said with an exaggerated wink.

Kaillie groaned. "This is why we have a bad reputation in town."

"Why, because I go around doing my best to stop crimes? I can't see how that's a bad thing," Aunt Lucy said.

"Because you're supposed to be a respectable older woman in town, and instead you're going around pretending to be a superhero."

"I *am* a superhero," Aunt Lucy said. "At least, to these humans who don't understand that magic is real, I am. I've even got sidekicks. Even Batman only had Robin. I have *three* sidekicks."

"As long as we don't have to see you in Spandex," Leanne teased.

"Oh, you never know," Aunt Lucy replied. "Besides, I'm fairly certain I'm not the only person in town looking into the murder." She looked directly at me as she said this, and I was fairly certain my heart stopped for a second. How on earth could she know?

Luckily, neither one of my cousins picked up on it. I didn't want anyone else to know what I was doing. This was my problem, and my problem alone. I liked Leanne and Kaillie, I just wasn't used to bringing other people into the fold. I was the sort of person who did things by themselves. Well, and with Dad. But he was gone now.

Trust just wasn't something that came to me easily.

"Alright," Leanne said, leaning in, her eyes gleaming. "Who did it then?"

"Well that's the thing, I haven't gotten quite that far yet," Aunt Lucy said.

"Can't you just cast a spell on someone?" I asked. "I mean, there has to be a spell that would force someone to tell you the truth, right?"

"Unfortunately, there's no spell that works that way," Aunt Lucy replied. "While it's possible to cast truth-telling spells, even a person under the influence of magic won't give away a secret so big it would cause them to get into major trouble; their subconscious won't allow it."

"Well, that certainly makes things harder than they needed to be," I muttered.

"I agree," Aunt Lucy said.

"I still can't believe you're doing this," Kaillie muttered. "Seriously, *one* of us is trying to be good enough to get invited back into the paranormal world, and it feels like at every turn you're undermining all of my efforts to show that we're not a family of bad people."

"What could possibly be better than solving a crime the local law enforcement doesn't have a hope of figuring out themselves?" Aunt Lucy asked. "Besides, half the town already thinks Eliza did it, so it's not like we're a ringing endorsement of people who have done the right thing right now. If anything, the three of you should be joining me in trying to solve this. The sooner everyone knows who did it, the better."

I slunk low in my seat as the waitress came over with our food. She looked at me carefully as she handed over my plate laden with a sandwich and fries, and I looked down at the ground, made all the more aware of my status as an outcast, as the new town resident who might have murdered someone.

I really hated this.

"So who do you think did it, then?" Leanne asked. "And where are the rest of the Floozies? I heard you were all together at the bank."

"Your mother had a doctor's appointment, and I think that place reeks like death," Aunt Lucy replied. "Dorothy had to get home to start a pot roast, and

Carmen had to go to work. So I decided to have a nice, peaceful lunch by myself. But to answer your question, I don't know yet. But I'll figure it out, don't you worry about that. Now, Eliza, I heard through the grapevine that you're learning a few simple spells."

"That's right," I replied. "Aunt Debbie has shown me how to change the color of things, and how to make them bigger and smaller."

"Good," Aunt Lucy said. "Those are the boring basics. I'll teach you real spells soon. When you girls are finished eating, I'm taking Eliza out for a bit of magic training."

"It's so unfair that I never get to learn magic," Leanne muttered.

"Don't teach her anything that the coven in the paranormal wouldn't approve of," Kaillie warned.

"Oh I wouldn't dream of it," Aunt Lucy replied with a mischievous smile. I had a sneaking suspicion that was exactly what I was about to be taught.

Eventually, the three of us finished eating, and Kaillie and Leanne went out to finish their errands, leaving Aunt Lucy and me sitting alone in the booth.

"Don't think I don't know you've also been looking into who killed Leonard."

"Who, me?" I asked, trying to look as innocent as possible. Aunt Lucy waved a finger at me in reply.

"Don't you 'who, me?' me, young lady," she replied. "I know perfectly well what it is you're doing, and why.

You don't want the whole town thinking you're a murderer."

"They already think that, I'm trying to prove that their opinions are wrong."

"Good. So you should. I know you went to see Don this morning; what do you think of him?"

I bit my lip, trying to decide how to answer. A part of me was still hesitant to ask for help, even though Aunt Lucy had already figured out what I was doing. I just really, really wasn't used to bringing other people into the fold when I did things. But at the same time, Aunt Lucy already figured out what I was doing. She obviously had no problem with it, and who knew? Maybe bouncing ideas off her could help me solve the crime after all.

"I think he's the killer," I finally replied in a low voice, glancing around to make sure no one at any of the nearby tables were able to listen in on the conversation. "I need proof, though. I was thinking of breaking into the store tonight and looking around. I'm hoping to find the ground wolfsbane he used to kill Leonard."

"Good," Aunt Lucy said. "You're thinking he's the killer because of his close relationship to Joe?"

"That's right," I said with a nod. "I have two different motives I'm working with, but they're both linked to the sale of that property. After all, people have been killed for less. Either Don killed him on behalf of Joe directly, in which case he acted as a hitman, or Don killed him with the hopes that Joe would spend a bunch of money at the hardware store when he was building the condos."

"I think you might be right," Aunt Lucy said. "None of us can find a reason Dianne might have had to kill Leonard."

"No, I can't see why she would have done it, either. She seemed to have just genuinely been nice to him. I guess the fact that they both worked at the bank was a coincidence."

"And it's the same with Jack Frost, the old math teacher," Aunt Lucy said. "I can't find any reason he would have had to be angry with Leonard."

"As far as I know, those are the only people who had the opportunity to kill him," I said with a shrug. "So it has to be Don."

"Agreed," Aunt Lucy said. "Now, all we need to do is prove it."

"So you agree? We need to search through his shop? I'm not the biggest fan of the idea, but I don't see how else we can do it."

"That's right," Aunt Lucy said. "In fact, I think we need to take care of it right now. You never know how long it's going to take for Don to get rid of the evidence."

I balked. "But I'm suggesting breaking into his store. A store he's going to be in. What on earth are you saying?"

Aunt Lucy winked. "You're a witch, remember?

We're going to use some magic. I told the other girls I was going to teach you the things Debbie wouldn't dare."

This didn't sound good. It *certainly* didn't sound legal.

CHAPTER 18

Aunt Lucy and I left the diner and made our way back down toward the street.

"So, what's the plan here?" I asked.

"I'm going to turn us both invisible," Aunt Lucy said. "We'll be able to sneak around the shop undetected, and look for the poison. But be careful: when you're invisible, anything you move will look like it's floating. Kaillie might be an overly-cautious ninny a lot of the time, but she is correct: the people in the paranormal world frown on it when we make our use of magic too obvious. That's why they sent Kyran the elf over the other day; the whole thing with the broom made a little bit too much noise."

"Wait, that was *me* they were upset about?" I asked. "I thought it was the whole thing with the donuts."

Aunt Lucy waved away my suspicions. "Goodness, no. There were two humans who saw that, and they both passed out. I'm sure they wrote it off as a concussion or something. However, hundreds of people saw you riding that broom through the middle of the mall. That's a little bit less conspicuous than the paranormal world is happy with."

My heart sunk as I realized I was in trouble not only in the human world, but in the paranormal one, too.

"Don't worry," Aunt Lucy said, as though reading my thoughts. She couldn't do that, could she? "I explained the whole situation to Kyran, and he told me he'd make sure the higher-ups in the coven understand that it was an accident, and that you didn't realize what you were doing."

"And you trust him?" I asked. "This elf?"

"Oh, implicitly," Aunt Lucy replied. "Kyran is very strange for an elf, by all accounts, but he's trustworthy."

"Alright," I said. "So I'm probably not in trouble in this magical world?"

"No, I don't think you are," Aunt Lucy said. "Now, are you going to keep doing your best impression of Kaillie, or are we going to find proof of a killer?"

I took a deep breath. Honestly, I wasn't completely sure I was ready for this. "Using magic?"

"That's right," Aunt Lucy said, dragging me down the alley next to the store. "You're going to have to get used to being around it, it might as well be now."

She pulled out her wand and pointed it at me. "Oh, and don't tell Debbie we did this. She's not a big fan of using magic to get away with committing felonies."

I gulped, hard. "Gee, I wonder why." I wasn't sure I was a big fan of it, either.

Still, this was the only way I could think of to find proof that Don had murdered Leonard, and clear my name for good.

I closed my eyes as Aunt Lucy began casting the spell. *"Saturn, god of wealth, make this witch invisible so she can move with stealth."*

When I opened my eyes a second later, I gasped as I looked down at myself. I wasn't there! I was literally just staring at concrete where my legs and torso had been a minute earlier.

I touched my face carefully, but I couldn't see my hands. They had to still be there somewhere, obviously, since my face could feel something touching it, but I couldn't see them.

"This is weird," I said, and Aunt Lucy laughed. "It takes some getting used to. Don't forget, you've lived on this planet for nearly a quarter decade and every single waking moment of that time you've been able to see your body. It's going to take your brain a bit of time to adjust to the fact that you're now invisible.

"No kidding," I replied as I took a cautious step forward. I wasn't entirely sure what was going to happen, but it was all normal. Well, apart from the whole part where I couldn't see anything.

Aunt Lucy repeated the spell, this time pointing the

wand at herself, and I gasped as she immediately disappeared.

"Alright, ready?" Aunt Lucy asked, and I nodded.

"Stay close to me, but don't speak too loudly," Aunt Lucy ordered. "We don't want any of the regular humans to pick up on the fact that we're here. That's the sort of thing that *will* get us in trouble in the paranormal world."

I nodded, before a split second later realizing that there was no way Aunt Lucy could see my reaction.

"Ok," I said. "Let's do this."

The two of us made our way toward the front door, but I reached out and grabbed Aunt Lucy's arm. At least, I really hoped that was her arm.

"Hang on," I said. "He has that bell that goes off above the main door. If we open it and there's no one there, he's going to start asking questions."

"Good thinking," Aunt Lucy whispered. "Here comes Alfred. He checks the hardware store for new sales literally every day. We'll sneak in just after him."

I didn't know who exactly Aunt Lucy was pointing at, but figured it was the older man making his way down the street with a bushy white beard and eyebrows that could have been used as a nest for small birds. He was dressed in paint-splattered overalls and made a beeline for the hardware store.

Sure enough, the man opened the front door, and Aunt Lucy and I slipped through immediately after him. I was sure no one would notice the fact that the door had stayed open for a tiny bit longer than it would have naturally.

As soon as I saw Don in front of the counter I took an involuntary breath in, but sure enough, he didn't notice me or Aunt Lucy at all. He was busy talking to Albert, who had gone straight to the front counter and was busy asking something about a sale on wood stain, and how Home Depot was running a sale and willing to ship to the island, so why couldn't Don?

Ok, this was a good sign. We hadn't been spotted yet. My instinct was to get as far away from Don and the front counter as possible, so I slipped down one of the aisles and toward the back of the store. I figured there might be an office or something back there; somewhere Don might have hidden the poison he used to kill Leonard.

The problem was the aisles in this store were so narrow it was a struggle not to touch anything on the way down. They were barely more than shoulder width, and I had never realized until now *just* how much noise it must be possible to make in a hardware store. The first part of this aisle was filled with tiny little boxes packed with dozens of screws of various sizes and with differently-shaped heads. If I accidentally knocked one over, it wouldn't be remotely subtle.

I turned myself sideways and slid carefully down the aisle, feeling a little bit like Pac-man. If I saw someone I was going to have to stop and go the other way, and if two people came at me in the same aisle from either direction, I was going to be caught.

Yes, this was basically a real-life version of Pac-man. I hadn't been the adventurous kid as a child, and I didn't handle stress very well. I had to stop and take a couple of deep breaths before I continued past a selection of spray paint kept on a gated shelf, and finally reached the back of the store.

To my immense relief, there was a door labeled 'Employees Only' against the back wall. That was exactly what I wanted and I stopped, my ears on high alert. From the front of the store, the sound of Don explaining to Albert that he didn't price match and never had reached my ears, and I knew it was safe to go inside. I tried the door and was relieved to find it unlocked. Small towns had their advantages, I guess.

I didn't waste a second and slid into the back part of the store and closed the door again behind me, reaching over until I found the light switch. A set of fluorescent lights slowly flickered to life overhead, and I found myself in the middle of a room that doubled as both an office and storage space.

Most of the room was packed with extra stock that wasn't on display, with items stacked from floor to ceiling across almost every single inch of the space. There were a few shelves, but most of the items were boxes, piled on top of one another so precariously that it reminded me of the world's biggest game of Jenga. Seriously, if someone made a wrong move in this place there was a good chance they were going to be crushed to death by an assortment of landline telephones, KitchenAid blenders, and Halloween decorations. Who on earth had their Halloween stuff ready to put out for sale in *April*? That was just ridiculous.

Even the "office" part of this room – which was really just a tiny desk in the corner – was piled high. All sorts of bills and other official-looking papers were stacked on top of the desk, one particularly large pile looming precariously close to the edge. Personal organization was obviously not Don Kilmer's strong suit.

I looked around, trying to figure out where to start. After all, I had some poison to find.

CHAPTER 19

I started off by making my way toward the desk. It seemed like both the least dangerous place to start, and also a likely place for the ground wolfsbane to be kept.

What did ground wolfsbane even look like? It had to be a powder. I reached into my pocket and pulled out my phone, intending to do a Google image search to help me figure out what I was looking for, and sighed. Of course my phone was also invisible; it had been in my pocket when Aunt Lucy cast the spell. Great.

Well, in a place like this, anything powdery and suspicious would probably be enough, I figured. I sat down on the chair, pretending to be Don, and asked myself where I would hide the poison if it were me.

I carefully checked under various piles of paper,

doing my best to put them back exactly as I found them. I assumed there wouldn't have been too much wolfsbane needed to kill Leonard; he had died so quickly, and he probably would have noticed if it was a large quantity that had been slipped into his coffee. So I might have been looking for even just a tiny Ziploc baggy full of a strange powder.

My eyes scanned, looking for something – anything – that might be poison, but instead they landed on a handwritten letter, piled underneath a few other sheets of paper. This sheet in particular stood out to me thanks to the handwritten aspect. Every single other sheet on this table was typed out. And when my eyes landed on the signatory at the bottom of the page and saw it was a letter from Leonard, my heart stopped for a second.

I grabbed at the sheet and immediately began scanning the words.

Don,

I know you're plotting with that bastard Joe to get my land. It's not going to work. The land belongs to nature, not for you to build your stupid condos on. You'll get that land over my dead body, so tell your friend the developer to just give up now. It's not worth it. If you keep trying, I'll make your life a living hell.

Leonard

Wow. This was definitely something. I looked around, desperate to see a photocopier, but there wasn't one. So instead, I plucked my phone out of my pocket, swiped the screen to the left to activate the camera, and took a picture. Hopefully even though the phone was invisible the picture would still work. After all, I'd taken so many pictures with this phone I basically knew off by heart where the button to press was. I really hoped I'd done it right.

This letter was fairly damning. If anything, it showed that Leonard was threatening the men trying to get the land sold. I wondered what it was he had planned. Maybe this letter was what had triggered Joe and Don – or possibly just Don – to decide that Leonard needed to be silenced permanently. I looked at the paper, quickly flipping it over, but didn't see any indication as to when the letter had been written. For all I knew, Leonard might have written it six months ago. Still, I doubted it. The letter was the fourth sheet down in a pile right on the top of the computer; assuming the pieces of paper on top were the newer ones, and going by the dates of a couple of invoices on the sheets above and below the letter, Don would have received this about a week ago.

I bit my lip as I read the letter again, trying to ignore the fact that it looked like it was floating in midair. What if Don had received this letter, read it, decided that it was time to get rid of Leonard once and for all before he became too much of an issue? What if he was worried that Leonard would go to any lengths to stop the land from being sold? After all, that letter was pretty obviously a threat.

What if that was what triggered all of this?

I put the letter back and slipped the phone back into my pocket, really hoping that the picture had worked. I hadn't found the poison, but I had at least found something that might help prove Don was the killer. And I still had the entire storage area to search as well. It was so big I knew I wasn't going to be able to check every nook and cranny like I'd done with the desk in the corner, but I could still check all of the boxes for signs that any of them had been opened, maybe to sneak some poison into them, or something along those lines.

However, before I got a chance to do even that, the door opened and Don came in. My eyes widened and I instinctively rushed away from him, toward the stacks of boxes, desperately hoping that he wasn't going to come in here.

"Give me a second, I know I have that invoice in here somewhere," he called out to someone back in the main shop.

Great. Great, great, great. Hopefully he was just going to walk in, immediately find the piece of paper he was after, and then leave. I held my breath as I slipped into a sort of aisle made up of giant cardboard boxes storing various things. I had obviously made my way into the section where Don stored the appliances; stacked to my left were a number of washer and dryers, and to my right were a couple of dishwashers, topped with piles of smaller kitchen appliances like toaster ovens, microwaves and blenders.

I made my way as far down the makeshift aisle as I could as Don shuffled through the pile of papers. Had I put everything back just the way it was? Could he tell someone had come through here and messed with his things? I hadn't even checked for a security camera. What if there was video footage somewhere of pieces of paper in Don's office randomly shuffling themselves? He was going to look over the footage and think there was a ghost.

A moment later, I heard the door to the main store open and close once more. "I got it right here," Don's voice called out, getting fainter as the door closed, and I immediately heaved a giant sigh of relief. I knew he couldn't see me, but I was absolutely terrified of getting caught all the same.

I briefly wondered if maybe I hadn't tempted fate just a little bit too much. Maybe it was time for me to sneak back into the main shop and get out of here.

But another part of me thought about going to jail for the rest of my life, and I nixed that idea. I was here, I was invisible, so why shouldn't I do my absolute best to find any remaining poison Don might have hidden?

Unfortunately, the universe had other ideas. About fifteen seconds later I heard the door open again. I paused, frozen in place, hoping it was Don just looking for another piece of paper, but no luck.

"I know I have one of those microwaves in here somewhere," he muttered to himself, and my blood went ice cold as he made a beeline straight for me.

I looked over to my right, where there sat a giant pile of microwaves. Don started heading toward me, and I panicked. I was trapped in a makeshift aisle. There were boxes to my left and right, behind me only the far wall. And Don was standing between me and the only way out of here. I looked to the ceiling.

Only one way to go from here.

As Don moved slowly toward me, checking the various microwaves, I climbed up onto one of the boxes to my left. I inched my way upwards, doing my absolute best to be as quiet as possible while Don muttered to himself.

"I know I've got one of them back here. Panasonic, Panasonic, LG, Black and Decker…"

I eventually managed to slip myself into a small gap between a couple of boxes, ensuring that Don wouldn't be able to notice me unless he specifically put his hand in that small gap. But there was no reason for him to do that at all.

On the other hand, the gap was tiny, uncomfortable, and my hamstrings were cramping up pretty badly given my awkward position. I closed my eyes and took the quietest deep breath that I could, telling myself it would all be over in a minute. Don was going to find the microwave, and he would get out of there, and I would be free to resume my search without the back of my leg feeling like it was being stabbed.

What I didn't realize was that my body pressing against the washer at my feet was slowly moving it forward, inch by inch. I thought my body was getting used to the cramped position, when the reality was it was simply making the hole bigger by pushing the boxes in front of me away.

It wasn't until the hole got so big that the box above fell down onto me that I realized what had happened.

By some miracle I managed not to cry out, and just held my arms above my head to protect my face. The box hit my body and rolled off, moving toward Don.

"What the-" I heard him call out before the box hit him. I glanced over just in time to see the box knock Don off balance and directly into the pile of appliances on the other side of the makeshift aisle.

I squeezed my eyes shut, not wanting to watch as all of the appliance boxes were knocked over as Don ran into them. The cacophonous sound of cardboard falling to the ground filled my ears, and when the sound finally dissipated, I opened my eyes, checking to make sure Don was ok.

He hadn't been completely crushed by the boxes. Instead, they were piled mostly around him while he still stood standing in the middle. An inflatable Halloween jack-o-lantern with a hole at the bottom had fallen directly onto Don's head, and he looked comically ridiculous as he stood, surrounded by the boxes.

"Now how on earth did that happen?" he asked, his voice muffled by the sound of the jack-o-lantern. He reached up to get it off, but it was so big that he struggled with it, eventually losing his balance, tripping on a box, and falling face-first into the pile of boxes.

It took everything I had not to burst out laughing. The jack-o-lantern face rolled over onto his back.

"Well, my afternoon is going to suck now," he muttered. "Stupid Halloween decorations. Next year I'm putting this stupid piece of crap up for sale for ten bucks, surely someone will pick it up at that price."

Don struggled with the jack-o-lantern stuck on his head for a minute until it finally popped off, then he stood up and kicked it to the other end of the room as hard as he could. It must have been unsatisfying though; instead of flying across the room and hitting the back wall with a bang the jack-o-lantern just floated slowly away.

Just then, a face I didn't recognize opened the door and poked its head in. It was a man, in his late thirties.

"Everything alright back there, Don?" he asked. "I heard a bit of a commotion."

"All good, Ken, thanks," Don called out in reply. "Be out in a minute."

The door closed once more and Don hunted through the pile of appliances, grabbing a microwave from the pile. One side of the box was dented, so Don did his best to make the cardboard look normal again before climbing out from the wreckage and making his way back out into the main store.

I figured that was my cue to go. I wasn't about to stay back here when Don was undoubtedly going to return to put everything back to normal. I counted to ten once the door closed, then made my way back toward it, opening it just enough to peek through the crack and see there was no one around before sliding back through to the main part of the store.

My heart racing, it took literally every single ounce of willpower I had not to fly out of the front door and run as far as possible from the hardware store as possible. I was fairly certain causing a box to fall over and triggering an entire aisle's worth of boxes to collapse on the store owner qualified as a bad use of the invisibility spell.

The man was at the counter, with Don running everything through the till.

"There's a bit of a dent on this box, are you sure this one's ok?" the man asked, looking carefully at his new microwave.

"I'm sure it's fine, it came like that," Don lied. "If there's a problem, bring it back and I'll take care of it for you."

"Thanks, man. Have a good one."

"You too."

With that, the man left the store, his microwave in

tow, and I peeled out the door after him, sneaking out the same way I had come in.

I stood out in the street, watching as the man walked back toward his car with his brand-new microwave, and I realized there was a small problem.

"Aunt Lucy?" I called out as loudly as I dared.

I was met with silence.

CHAPTER 20

Alright, so Aunt Lucy and I probably should have come up with a plan to meet afterwards so she could reverse the spell. Of course, I'd have been way better off thinking of that an hour ago.

What on earth was I going to do now? I was here, in the middle of town, completely invisible, with no way of reversing the spell.

I supposed the best thing to do was wait and hope that I heard Aunt Lucy call out to me. So I hung around, loitering in front of the hardware store, feeling incredibly awkward about it but knowing that not a single one of the souls walking past had the least idea that I was there.

After about an hour passed – I assumed, since I didn't have any way to check on the actual time – I decided this was stupid. Aunt Lucy had probably left before me. Or maybe she was still in there. But either way, I was getting cold, impatient and uncomfortable.

I decided I had no other choice: I began walking back toward Aunt Debbie's house. Hopefully she was home by now.

Either way, I had done it. I hadn't found any extra poison, which would prove beyond a doubt that Don was the killer, but I had a photo of the letter Leonard had sent him that gave Don an extra reason to want Leonard dead – Leonard was threatening him.

And who knew, maybe Aunt Lucy had found the poison during her investigation as well. I wouldn't know until I found her again.

I was feeling pretty good about myself and the investigation as I made my way down Main Street toward Aunt Debbie's house. Eventually, I found myself walking behind two women that I didn't know, and I was just about to slip past them when I realized they were talking about the murder.

"Well, I was just speaking with Ron this morning," one of the women said. "You know, he's never been the sharpest tool in the shed, but he gets there eventually."

"Most of the time, anyway," her companion replied dryly.

"I told him he had to watch that new girl. You know she's related to Lucy Marcet? There's something not right about that family, I'm telling you. She's the one who served him the coffee. She had the best chance at poisoning him."

"Right," the other woman said. "I hope he took you seriously."

"Oh, he did," the first woman said. "He told me he had people already looking into her, and that they were going to be interviewing her shortly. He told me he didn't like the way new people were constantly coming into town, and how crime seemed to constantly be going up. Ever since he became police chief, he said, the crime rate's gone up, and it's got to be because of all these newcomers. He doesn't like them, and so he's going to be taking a good, hard look at that new girl."

My heart sunk. Obviously, they were talking about me. Well, thank goodness I now had that piece of paper that showed Don had an extra reason to want Leonard dead.

"Good. I mean, I'm not sure it's the out-of-towners that are the problem," the other woman replied. "After all, it could just be the fact that as nice as Ron is, he's completely incompetent. I think that's probably got more to do with the increase in crime than anything else. As for the new girl, well, she might have been born here, but you're right, she's an outsider. You never know."

"Plus, I was talking to Ron about the case. He was telling me that Don, his brother-in-law, was one of the people suspected. Can you imagine? Don! Of course, I told Ron that was ridiculous, and he agreed with me, told me there isn't a chance of Don spending a single night in jail. But when your suspects are people like

Don Kilmer, well, I think it becomes obvious who the more likely murderer is."

"Certainly not Don," the other woman agreed. "Why, he's been a stalwart of the community for years. It's not just anybody who can run the local hardware store."

"Did you hear his daughter is going out with Ryan and Annette's daughter?" the woman said. "Those two would make just the most wonderful couple."

"I did hear that! They've been friends for years, so it's not really a surprise."

As the conversation moved on I stopped and let the two women continue on. I hadn't realized that Don Kilmer was the brother-in-law of the police chief here in town. That was going to make it *way* harder to get him arrested. I really hoped Aunt Lucy had found the poison in his store somewhere, because otherwise things were not looking good.

I ended up at Aunt Debbie's about fifteen minutes later and knocked on the door. She opened it a minute later and looked around, a little bit confused.

"Hi Aunt Debbie, it's me," I said in a small voice, a little bit embarrassed.

"Eliza? Where are you?"

"I'm right in front of you, but I'm invisible."

Aunt Debbie frowned. "Let me guess. Lucy?"

"Yeah," I replied.

"Alright, hang on one second." Aunt Debbie pulled

out a wand, muttered a spell, and a split second later as I looked down, I was completely back to normal.

"Wow!" I said. "That is pretty cool."

"Now, what on earth did you do to get Aunt Lucy to turn you invisible?"

"Umm…" I started. I had a sneaking suspicion Aunt Debbie wasn't going to be too pleased if I told her the truth, that we were investigating Leonard's murder by ourselves and were trying to find proof Don Kilmer was the killer. "Is it ok if I keep it to myself?"

Aunt Debbie smiled at me. "Of course it is. But listen, if you're ever in trouble, for any reason, please know that you can come to me. I realize you're in the middle of a very difficult transition, and that it can't be easy with both of your parents gone. I know you barely know me, but no matter what, I will have your back. I promise."

"Thanks, Aunt Debbie," I said with a smile. I did really appreciate how hard she was working to make me feel welcome here in Enchanted Enclave Island.

"Now, do you want to head back into town, or are you going to hang around here until dinner?"

"I think I've had enough adventures for one day," I said with a smile. "I think I might have a quiet rest of the afternoon."

"Perfect, that sounds good," Aunt Debbie replied. "The rest of the family is coming over for dinner, so we'll have company. Tonight is pork chops."

"Sounds good, thanks!" I said.

Dinner around the table was hectic. Aunt Lucy showed up a bit late, and winked at me.

"Well, Don didn't have any poison in his store," she announced to everyone as soon as we were all settled around the dining table. "But I still think he's the one who killed Leonard."

Kaillie groaned. "Don't tell me you actually went in and searched his store."

"It's ok; it's not like he knew what was happening."

"Well, that suddenly explains a lot," Aunt Debbie said, looking pointedly at me. I blushed and quickly began scooping mashed potatoes onto my plate.

"I didn't realize Don was the police chief's brother-in-law," I said. "I overheard a couple of women saying that this afternoon."

"That's right," Uncle Robert said with a nod. "Chief Ronald is married to Don's sister, Marianne."

"That's the reason why I was looking for poison," Aunt Lucy said. It was nice of her not to give me away. "Anything less than the equivalent of a smoking gun and Don's going to sneak through the fingers of the law on the basis that he married a woman with the right last name. She's perfect for Ronald, though. You can look in one ear and out the other with that one."

Leanne and Kaillie began to snicker, and Aunt

Debbie shot Aunt Lucy a look. "You're setting a bad example for the girls."

"Oh please, they're adults now. I'm sure they're very aware that some of the other adults in town aren't the brightest bulbs in the hardware store."

"She's right, Auntie," Leanne said. "Besides, even if we hadn't already known that Marianne Kilmer was an idiot, we would have gotten a pretty solid hint when she married Ron."

Aunt Debbie looked disapprovingly at Aunt Lucy all the same, who was busy cutting up a piece of pork and doing her absolute best to avoid her sister's gaze.

I realized that I hadn't actually checked my phone to see if I'd taken the picture properly. I pulled it out and opened up the photo app, and was thrilled to find that while I hadn't gotten it completely straight, the letter that Leonard had written to Don was there.

"What would you have done if you did find something, out of curiosity?" I asked Aunt Lucy. "Maybe not the poison, but something else that could be pertinent to the case."

Aunt Lucy understood my meaning immediately. "Well, it depends. Would I have left it there to be found, or taken it?"

"Hmm," I said, pretending to ponder the question. "Let's say left it there, but took a photo of it."

"I'd probably show it to one of the cops, but not to Ron," Aunt Lucy said. "Or maybe send it to someone I trusted and get them to do it."

"Please, since when have you ever let anybody do something for you?" Leanne scoffed with a laugh.

"She's not talking about herself," Kaillie said, looking at me. "Did you seriously join our aunt in this terrible idea?"

I shrugged. "Everyone in town thinks I killed Leonard. Apparently, the chief of police is an idiot with no chance of solving this, so if I want to stay here without being "that girl who got away with killing one of the most infamous people in town" I had better make sure the case gets solved."

Kaillie groaned. "And here I was hoping you'd be yet another ally in the fight to get us allowed back into the paranormal world."

"Don't worry, I didn't actually use magic. Aunt Lucy did that. The only thing I can do right now is change the color of things, and make them either bigger or smaller."

"Still, it's the principle of it," Kaillie said. "You shouldn't be going around trying to solve murders. That's not what good witches do."

"Well, wouldn't it be better for me to solve the case? If I get arrested and charged with Leonard's murder, or even if I just get investigated, wouldn't that make me look like way worse of a person?"

"Yeah, I guess," Kaillie replied, biting her lip. "I guess I never thought about it that way."

"I want to know why I wasn't invited to come join," Leanne said, leaning forward. "And Aunt Lucy was using magic? Just because I'm not a witch doesn't mean I don't want to be involved. Aunt Lucy can cast all the magic for me."

"Did I really raise you to be the type of young woman who goes around solving crimes?" Uncle Bob asked, turning to Leanne.

"You raised me to fight for what I want and take no crap for anyone, so I think this counts."

"Yeah, I guess that's fair," Uncle Bob replied with a shrug. "Do what you want, but don't get arrested or we'll have to find someone else to work as a barista."

I couldn't help but smile; Dad would have *never* reacted that way. Uncle Bob seemed like the most laid-back guy I'd ever met, and yet I knew that for him and Aunt Debbie to have successfully started a company from the ground up he had to be a pretty smart guy. Still, if I'd ever told Dad I was going to get myself embroiled in a murder investigation, I knew he wouldn't have been as calm as Uncle Bob.

"Good," Leanne said with a grin. "Now, what did you find, and what's the next step?"

"Do we really have to talk about this at the dinner table?" Aunt Debbie asked, and she was met with a resounding "Yes!" from her nieces and one of her sisters, so she threw up her hands. "Fine. But Robert is right. No one gets arrested. And Lucy, for goodness sake, the next time you cast an invisibility spell on your niece either make sure she knows how to reverse it or plan ahead on how you're going to reverse it. You're lucky she had the good sense to come here and get me to do it."

"It's not my fault; it's been ages since I'd had to cast invisibility spells on someone who doesn't have magical powers. The last time was when Leanne was in high… I mean, never mind."

I looked over at Leanne to see her glaring at her Aunt. "That's right, never mind. I definitely never used Aunt Lucy's magic for anything nefarious when I was in high school."

I grinned into the mouthful of sautéed green beans I shoved into my mouth as no one at the table decided to pursue the subject.

"Alright, so now that it's all out in the open, what did you find?" Aunt Lucy asked me from across the table.

"There was a letter in the office at the back," I explained. "It was from Leonard, to Don." I pulled out my phone and read the contents of the letter aloud to the table.

"Well, that's a pretty solid reason for him to kill Leonard," Leanne said. "He would have wanted to get Leonard off his back. The guy might have killed Leonard before Leonard did something crazy. I mean, we all know he could be a bit weird."

"Oh?" I asked.

"A couple of years back Leonard threw a bunch of black paint on an oil executive who came to town," Uncle Bob explained. "That was the most recent event I know of. He was arrested and spent the night in jail, but the oil executive declined to press charges. He said he just wanted to enjoy the rest of his holiday with his family."

"Sounds like Leonard was pro-environment," I said. "But yeah, maybe Don thought about things like that and decided he didn't want to be Leonard's next target. Or maybe Joe found out about it and hired Don to take care of things."

"Either way, it's pretty good evidence," Aunt Lucy said. "You should tell the cops about it when you get the chance. I just wish I'd found the poison."

"Me too," I said. I did a decent check in the back room."

"There was a bit of a crash that came from there a little while after you went in, did you have anything to do with that?"

"A crash? No, I don't know anything about that," I lied, shaking my head and doing my best to look as innocent as possible.

CHAPTER 21

With the coffee shop opening again on Wednesday I made my way in with Aunt Debbie once more, with Leanne and Kaillie arriving just after us.

"You should move in with us when you're ready," Leanne told me as she got the coffee machine ready for the day. "We have tons of space. Aunt Debbie is nice and all, but we're way more fun."

"Thanks," I said. "I might take you up on that soon." Honestly, a part of me was resisting because I didn't want to change my living situation yet again only to find myself arrested, accused of murder, or simply made the town pariah. I was warming up to life here, and while I really hated the situation that had led to my being here, it was kind of nice having such a big family now. Different, for sure. But nice.

Uncle Robert poked his head in through the door

leading to the industrial side of the business. "Hey, when you girls see Deb can you let her know I need a hand with the computer back here? Thanks."

"Sure, I'll go grab her now," I said, making my way to the kitchen at the back. I passed on the message, then looked at the platters of delicious-looking baked goods that had just come out of the oven.

"These smell amazing," I said to Kaillie, who grinned.

"Thanks! I was thinking that I want to expand our baked offerings here at the café. All we sell right now are basic muffins and donuts, and I want to be a bit more experimental."

"Oh, that's a good idea."

"I have a whole Pinterest board filled with recipes I want to try. That one there is a raspberry cheesecake crumb cake."

I gazed at the luscious cake, which was cooling on a wire rack, and my mouth began drooling involuntarily.

"Do you ever use magic when you're baking?" I asked Kaillie, and she shook her head.

"No. I don't think it's fair that people should have magically enhanced goods given to them when they're not expecting it. Of course, I do use some magic here and there to help things along. It's way easier to measure out flour with a spell than it is to do it by hand, or to get butter from the fridge. But that's all I do."

"What kind of enhancements can you do with magic?" I asked.

"Oh, tons of things. Most of them are done with potions. You create a potion that has a certain effect on a person, and you add them into the dough. For most potions, changing their temperature through baking won't affect them whatsoever – you do have to be careful with a few that require temperature changes, but they're rare – and so the only thing you have to watch for is the consistency of the dough after you've added potions. I could, for example, make a potion that would increase your energy levels. But then seeing as I work in a coffee shop, that's probably counter-intuitive. There are also potions that can make you feel happier, that can reduce anxiety, that can create laser focus, that can soothe anger, all sorts of things.'

"Wow," I said, my eyebrows rising. "I had no idea. You know, you could probably make some super cool muffins and stuff for people if you added the potions in."

"I know, I've thought about it before," Kaillie said. "But then, I always come back to the fact that none of these people would know what I had done. I feel like giving people magical potions without their knowledge – even if I do advertise the fact that the goods would have an effect – isn't fair to people. And of course, I can't admit it's done with magic. So I figure it's best to not do it at all."

"What about when you bake for family and stuff?" I said with a grin.

"Oh, I've been tempted to slip a sleeping potion into Aunt Lucy's stuff a few times, let me tell you," Kaillie said. "I like to tell myself it's for the good of the whole town. But no, I don't do that, either. Using magic sneakily is not using magic well."

"Fair enough. Will you show me one day how to make these potions?"

"Of course," Kaillie said, her eyes brightening. "I actually really enjoy potion-making. I think it's because it's so similar to baking. I'd love to teach you the basics."

Her enthusiasm was contagious, and I found myself looking forward to learning how to make potions. After all, there were quite a few things on that list that I'd love to have access to. A potion that could make you happy? Give you energy? Make you forget your anxiety? Yes, please!

I would be all over that in an instant.

I made my way back out to the main part of the coffee shop, and a few minutes later flipped the sign on the front door and unlocked it, ready to welcome our customers for the day.

"So, your mom is one of Lucy's Floozies?" I asked Leanne. "How do you feel about that?"

Leanne grinned. "I think it's hilarious. Mom met Aunt Lucy through Dad. She was always a bit of an independent spirit, so she naturally gravitated toward the crazy that is Aunt Lucy. They were friends throughout the marriage, and when mom and dad split up, mom kept Aunt Lucy as one of her best friends."

"I'm glad that worked out, and there don't seem to be any hard feelings between Aunt Lucy and Uncle Bob."

"Don't get me wrong, there were for a while. For about a year Uncle Bob refused to talk to Aunt Lucy, accused her of betraying him when he was just trying to do what was best for his family. But he eventually got over it. Dad doesn't really hold grudges very well."

"Do your parents get along now? Sorry, don't answer if that's too sensitive."

Leanne shrugged. "Don't worry, it's hard to come up with a topic so sensitive I won't talk about it. They're fine. They don't really talk, but it's not like they're constantly fighting or at each other's throats or anything. They're both, well, being adults about it."

"That's good," I said. "I'm glad you're not stuck in the middle of a nasty divorce."

"No, I was fifteen when they separated, so I was already old enough to understand what was going on," Leanne said, but before she could say anymore, Janice walked in, this time wearing leggings and a tight tank top, a water bottle in her other hand.

"Namaste, Eliza," she greeted me with a smile.

"Namaste," I said in reply, taking her re-usable coffee cup and passing it over to Leanne, who began making her regular order.

"The universe is telling me I should get a muffin to go with that coffee this morning," Janice told me, carefully eyeing the goods on display.

"Did the universe suggest a flavor?" I asked with a small smile.

"She's leaving that up to me," Janice said. "I'm thinking lemon poppy seed. Could I get that to go?"

"Sure," I said, opening up a bag and carefully taking the biggest muffin we had and putting it in that one. I worked under the concept of "the early bird gets the worm". So long as the early bird was polite, that was. Rude birds, no matter how early they came in, always got the smallest worms. Or in this case, the smallest muffins.

"Thanks, ladies," Janice said when Leanne finished making her coffee, holding up the cup in salute as she left the shop.

The next customer who walked through the door was far less welcome, as far as I was concerned. It was the police officer who took my statement the day Leonard died, Ross Andrews.

"Hi," he greeted me as he came up to the counter. I couldn't help but notice the dimples that appeared in his cheek when he smiled, and the way his eyes glimmered, as if he was just happy to be alive.

"Hi there, what can I get you?"

"I was hoping to have a chat with you, actually," he said. "I have a few questions to ask."

"Right now?" I asked, looking at Leanne.

"Go for it," she said. "I can handle things on my own for a few minutes, and I'll get mom to come back from helping Uncle Bob if I need it."

I nodded and made my way around the counter. "Do we have to go to the police station?" I asked, and Detective Andrews shook his head.

"Oh no, this is far less formal than that. We can just chat at one of the tables in the corner here if you'd like," he said, motioning toward a couple of them. I nodded and sat down, trying not to let my nerves show.

Was this just Detective Andrews trying to make me feel more comfortable before hitting me hard with questions intent to prove I was the killer? Should I insist on having a lawyer there? I just didn't know.

It was hard to think that this particular detective was about to lull me into a trap, though. He opened up his notebook casually and grabbed a pen, but the way he looked at me was kind, like he knew what I was going through and just wanted to get through this as quickly and painlessly as possible for the both of us.

But maybe that was just what he wanted me to think. I did know that every time I looked at him butterflies fluttered inside my stomach, but I forced myself not to think about that. I couldn't think about it, especially not right now.

"So, Eliza," he said, flipping to a new page and getting his pen ready. "I just wanted to run over some things with you."

"Ok," I replied.

"First of all, you said you didn't know Leonard Steele before you served him the morning he died?"

"That's right," I replied with a nod. "I had only arrived in town the day before. Everyone who came in that day I met for the first time."

"Have you ever visited Enchanted Enclave before you came to live here?"

"No," I said, shaking my head. "Well, I was born here, but we moved away when I was a baby. I don't remember this place at all."

Detective Andrews gave me a questioning look. "Really? You never once came to visit family when you were younger?"

I shook my head. "No. Dad never told me about this side of the family. My mom died when I was a baby, and that was when he left. It was only now, when my dad died, that my mom's family found me and told me about this place."

"Ok," Detective Andrews said, scribbling into his notepad. "So I'm guessing you had no reason whatsoever to have a grudge against Leonard?"

I shook my head. "Same answer as last time, detective, sorry. I didn't know him, I didn't know anything about him, I had nothing against him."

"Alright," Detective Andrews said. "Thanks. Do you know of anything else that might help us solve this case?"

I was about to open my mouth to tell him about

what I'd found in the hardware store – although I had yet to come up with a good reason as to where I would have come up with the letter – when another man approached the table. I had seen him at the crime scene, although I hadn't been introduced to him. Medium height, with a beer belly that he liked to stick out to make himself seem more important, beady black eyes and a balding head with wisps of reddish-brown looked down at me. I wasn't completely sure, but a part of me felt like I could smell beer on him.

"Right, this the server girl?" he asked. His voice was low and gravelly.

"This is Eliza Emory, yes," Detective Andrews replied, fidgeting slightly in his chair.

"Good. I wanted to talk to her."

"And you are?" I asked, and the man scoffed.

"Ronald Jones, Chief of Police here at Enchanted Enclave," he replied, grabbing a chair from a nearby table and sitting down with us. "I've been meaning to speak with you, Eliza. Now, why isn't this conversation taking place at the station, Ross?"

Detective Andrews shrugged. "I didn't see a need for it. Her initial statement says that she was new in town and didn't know Leonard at all. Her statement now backs that up, so why would I drag her in to the station for an interview when I could just do it here? Especially since this way she doesn't have to leave her job in the middle of the day on a whim."

"Because it's not just about the reality, it's about

appearances," the police chief growled. "Half this town thinks she did it, so we need to bring her in to make it look like we're getting the job done."

"Ah, yes, because that's so much easier than actually doing the job," Detective Andrews replied, looking his boss straight in the eye, and I had to admit, I was impressed. He was obviously right, and I wasn't just saying that because Chief Jones had just said to my face what I had secretly known. It was better for the police to actually find the real killer rather than pretend they were looking into someone.

"Well, just because you've gotten that information doesn't make it correct," the police chief replied. "Now, lookie here, girl. You say you didn't know Leonard Steele?"

"No, I didn't know him," I replied firmly. "The first time I saw him, the first time I met him, was when he came in to order the coffee."

"Then why did you kill him?"

"I didn't!" I exclaimed instinctively, blood draining from my face. For all the rumors that had been going around, no one had *actually* accused me of killing Leonard yet. At least, not directly to me.

"How do we know that? Everyone in town seems to think you did it."

"Well, everyone in town is wrong, then," I answered, crossing my arms. "I didn't have any reason to kill Leonard, and I didn't have any way to kill Leonard either."

"You're one of the Marcet family, aren't you?"

"That was my mom's maiden name, yes."

"Well, they're a weird bunch, those ones. Wouldn't put it past one of you to have ground whatever-that-poison-was-called."

I stared at him incredulously. "Seriously? Just because my family can be a bit weird you're going to try and pin this on me?"

"Yes, sir, come on," Detective Andrews said. "This is getting ridiculous. We have absolutely no evidence that Eliza is the killer, beyond the fact that she had the opportunity to kill Leonard, and no reason to think she would have done it."

"You might not, but I know for a fact that none of the other people with the opportunity would have done it, either," Chief Jones said, his voice rising. I glanced around to see the couple of customers at other tables staring toward us, and I did my best to sink low into my seat, as far away from view as I could.

Here I was, being accused of murder by the chief of police in town, in full view of a handful of people. This was not going to do wonders for my reputation.

"Well then find someone else," I said. "Because I didn't do it."

"*Someone* did it," Chief Jones replied. "And frankly, I'm more inclined to believe the newcomer to town than people I've known for years and years."

"Well, what you believe and what reality dictates are often two different things," I said, crossing my arms. I wasn't normally the type of person to stand up to authority like this, but this was my *life* we were talking about. And here was Chief Jones, talking about locking me up for murder like he was just looking to do it because it made his life more convenient.

"I agree with Eliza," Detective Andrews said. "Come on, Chief. We've bothered her enough for now. Let's let her get back to work, we'll work this case some more, and if we find any more reason to talk to her we'll do it, but not until then."

"Fine, fine," the chief muttered, struggling to get out of his chair. I had a sneaking suspicion he actually *had* been drinking. But jeez, it was barely ten in the morning.

Detective Andrews shot me an apologetic glance as he led the Chief out the door, and I found myself lost in thought as I made my way back to the counter.

CHAPTER 22

"I see you've finally had the pleasure of meeting our esteemed chief of police," Leanne said, rolling her eyes when I made my way back behind the counter.

"Yeah," I said, blowing a bunch of air from my cheeks. "I could have done without that conversation. He thinks I'm the one who killed Leonard, because he doesn't believe it could be anyone else that he knows."

"Sounds about right. Look, I know it seems hopeless, but he's not the only cop in town. Most of the others are at least somewhat decent at their jobs. Heck, Ross Andrews is actually pretty good at it. So as long as he's on the case, you're probably going to be fine. Remember, Chief Jones can arrest you, but that doesn't mean you're going to be convicted."

"Gee, that's a reassuring thought."

"Sorry. I just don't want you to give up hope."

"I know. It's also that he actually stated that everyone in town thinks I'm the killer. If I don't find the real killer, how can I ever make a life here? Fifty years from now people will still be talking about me as 'that woman who killed Leonard Steele'."

"Well, that's why we're all working together to help solve this," Leanne said. "We're your family. We stick together, and we're going to do what's right."

I smiled at Leanne. It was so nice of her to say that. But a part of me still resisted. I knew that this side of the family had welcomed me with open arms, and that they were willing to help with anything I needed, and I was eternally grateful to them for that. But there was a part of me – the part of me that had spent my whole life alone, apart from my dad – that resisted the idea. I could do it all by myself. It was always me and Dad, and now it was just me. I could do it. I had to do it myself.

And I was going to do it. I just wasn't entirely sure how, yet.

※

During my lunch break I wanted to head down to the beach, but the one I knew was just a bit too far away.

"Are there any nearby beaches where I can eat lunch?" I asked Leanne, who nodded.

"Sure. Take the alley between the post office and the

ice cream shop next to it. Just past the buildings it becomes a path. You're five minutes from the beach there. It's a nice one, too, since it's on the south side of the island so it's not completely exposed to the Pacific winds. The water is a bit calmer. It's still way too cold to swim, of course, but it's a nice place to spend a sunny day like this."

"Thanks," I said with a smile, grabbing a slice of the raspberry crumb cake to eat for lunch and giving her a quick wave. I checked my phone for the time, and then followed her instructions. Sure enough, just past the buildings was a narrow dirt trail that led through the trees and eventually opened up onto a nice beach. It was smaller than the one I'd been to before, and with more trees around, less windy. It was actually quite nice, and I found myself hoping that I'd be able to spend a lot of days on this beach in the future.

I was alone on the beach once more, and I made my way toward the water. The wet sand indicated that the tide was going out rather than coming in, so I found a rock close to the water that had mostly dried and sat down on top of it, taking my slice of cake out of the little bag and getting ready to enjoy it.

Taking a first heavenly bite, I savored the cake as I looked out over the water. I could see another couple of islands out on the horizon. A couple hundred yards away what looked like a seal, or maybe an otter was swimming in the water, poking its head up from time to time.

I smiled to myself; as much as I wanted to resist getting attached to this place, it was growing on me. Sure, it was colder than I was used to, and the ocean up here felt more wild than back home in California, but it was beautiful in its own way. On this island I felt more connected to nature, and I liked the feeling. I could actually really understand why Leonard Steele had wanted to fight the development of new condos on the beach.

But I couldn't allow myself to get attached. Not with this murder investigation hovering over my head. After all, I couldn't live in a town where half the population thought I was a murderer. That just wasn't a viable long-term option for me. I'd be better off moving to Siberia in that case.

At least the delicious cake was taking the sting out of the reality of my situation. Though, if I had to move, I'd never be able to get more of it. That thought was disappointing.

Suddenly, I spotted something out in the water, about fifty, maybe seventy feet from shore. At first I thought it was a piece of seaweed, but it wasn't moving with the current. In fact, it looked like it was trying to fight it.

I stood up to get a better look, squinting hard. Were those ears? What *was* that?

A small mew suddenly reached my ears and I gasped as I realized it came from the ocean. That was a cat! It had to be.

I dropped the rest of my cake on the sand and rushed toward the water, kicking off my shoes. I didn't even think. That was a cat out there, and it was in trouble. Another mew reached my ears, this one sounding more desperate. I ran straight into the water, letting out a yelp as soon as the frigid water hit my feet and ankles. Oh man, the water here was *way* colder than back in San Francisco. I paused for a second, jumping in place, then looked out at the cat once more.

"Ohhhh, this is going to be cold," I said out loud to no-one as I ran in, squealing the entire time, doing my best to keep my eyes on the cat.

"Let me just save this poor thing before I die of hypothermia," I said as my teeth began to chatter. I was waist-deep now, and still about thirty feet from the cat. It was facing away from me, and couldn't see me.

As I made my way deeper and deeper, I knew I was going to have to start swimming. I decided to just get it over with. Pushing with my legs I dropped my upper body into the water.

"Eeeeeeeeee!" I cried out as the frigid water reached my neck. I struggled to breathe; my throat didn't want to let any air in. Every inch of my body felt like it was being stabbed by tiny shards of ice. The waves were bigger here, one caught me by surprise and my mouth filled with salt water, which I struggled to spit out.

I had never been a strong swimmer; I'd taken a few lessons as a kid, enough to be able to make it from one end of the pool to the other without drowning, but I wasn't big on swimming and this was altogether much rougher conditions than I was used to.

For a split second I lost sight of the cat, and I was worried that he had sunk, but the waves shifted again and I saw him.

"I'm here," I managed to stammer though chattering teeth as I reached the cat. His eyes were half-closed; it was a miracle he was still above the water. "I'm here, I've got you."

I flipped onto my back and held the cat close to my chest as I began kicking back toward shore. I couldn't feel my arms or my feet anymore, so I watched the cat to make sure I didn't drop it back in the water.

"It's going to be ok," I whispered to the poor thing, hoping I wasn't lying. As soon as we got back to shore I looked around. There was nothing here to keep it warm, so I just started running. I had never been this cold in my life, but I knew I had to do something quickly to save this cat's life.

CHAPTER 23

By the time I reached the coffee shop again, I was completely out of breath. I ran in and Leanne gaped at me.

"What on earth happened?"

"I'll explain later," I said, rushing past the crowd of curious customers and straight into the kitchen. Kaillie looked up at me from where she stood in front of a giant mixer.

"Eliza! Are you ok?"

"This cat was in the water," I said quickly. "He's freezing, you have to save him."

"Of course." Kaillie didn't waste any more time asking questions, she grabbed her wand off the counter and pointed it at the cat. "*Saturn, god of generation, make this cat warm and dry, the perfect combination.*"

I gasped slightly as the cat's fur went from wet and matted to nice and puffed up, like he had just spent ten minutes under a hairdryer. He let out a weak mew, and I laughed.

"Oh, Kaillie, you saved him. Thank you!"

"No problem. Looks like you need the same spell." Kaillie repeated the words, and a second later I felt warmth coursing through me, like I had just stepped into a warm bath. Well, without the wetness. Sensation started to come back to my arms and legs, and I wiggled my fingers and toes as pins and needles ran through them. My hair probably looked like I'd just taken a bath with a toaster, and my clothes weren't dripping onto the floor anymore. "Look at you! I have a first aid kit back here, you're going to need it."

I looked down to see what Kaillie meant, and immediately realized what the problem was. By running barefoot back up the beach I had gone along the dirt path in my bare feet. I hadn't felt it at the time, but my feet were not only covered in bruises from stepping on dirt, stones and twigs, but they were bleeding as well.

Kaillie had already made her way to one of the cupboards at the back of the room and grabbed an unmarked plastic box. She opened it and pulled out some glass jars filled with strange-looking liquid.

"Are those magical potions?" I asked, looking at the liquids curiously. They were unlike anything I'd ever seen before. One of them looked like the colored part of lava lamps. The other looked like a light blue nail polish, and the third was completely clear, but with little blue dots floating in it.

"They are," Kaillie said with a nod, pulling the cork out from the first bottle. "Now sit on the table and show me your feet."

I did as she asked, carefully stroking the cat in my arms. Kaillie brushed the dirt off my now-dry feet, then poured the potion into her palm and began rubbing it on my skin.

I gasped as the cool liquid touched my skin. Not only was it a bit cold, but it caused a tingling sensation to run along my foot. And the cuts – I could see one of them on the side of my foot – suddenly disappeared.

"Wow!" I said, impressed. "Those cuts are just gone!"

"They are," Kaillie confirmed. "This potion is a staple of every first aid kit a witch has. As long as the cut isn't too big, it'll immediately heal over."

"How big is too big?" I asked.

"If it's a cut that would need more than a couple of stitches, that's too big," Kaillie said. "Then there are other magical options. But for small cuts and scrapes, this is perfect."

"Yeah, I can't believe it," I said.

"You do have one slightly bigger problem though," Kaillie said with a smile.

"Oh?"

"You can't go back out into the main serving area with your clothes, skin and hair being completely dried off three minutes after coming in here looking like a swamp monster."

"I think you mean like a sexy mermaid. But, point taken. What do I do?"

Kaillie bit her lip. "How attached are you to these clothes?"

I shrugged. "Not very."

"Good." She pulled out her wand and muttered something under her breath. A second later, the plain black pants and black shirt I'd been wearing had been changed into jeans and a cute sweater.

"Now that is just super cool," I said with a grin.

"It looks like you just got changed back here," Kaillie said, handing me a hair tie. "People will believe you were able to dry your hair, but maybe put it up in a ponytail or something, too."

"Alright," I said, moving to put the cat down so I could put my hair up. "Time to get up, little guy."

"First of all, no. I'm comfortable and I don't want to move. Secondly, I'm not a guy. Could someone this beautiful possibly be male? I didn't think so."

I almost dropped the cat.

"Did... did you hear that?" I asked Kaillie, who had already began making her way back toward the machine she'd been working at.

"Hear what?"

"Nothing, never mind," I said. I was going insane. I had to have imagined it. Maybe it was just my brain trying to recover from almost freezing to death in that water. I put the cat down, and he scowled at me. Actually maybe it was a girl after all. It *was* a gorgeous cat. Completely black except for one little patch of white on its back left paw, and with the most beautiful green eyes I had ever seen, the cat looked, well, majestic.

"Ugh. I said I didn't want to get up," the cat said, staring up at me, and I gaped at it.

"Kaillie?"

"Yeah?"

"You heard *that*, right?"

"Heard what?"

"This is going to sound insane, but I think the cat is talking to me."

"Of course I'm talking to you," the cat replied. "Stop treating me like I'm some sort of animal. It's patronizing, and a queen like myself deserves nothing but the utmost respect."

I closed my eyes and shook my head. "Nope. Nope, nope, nope. This can't be happening. You're not talking. Cats don't talk. Animals don't talk."

"Ugh, no one warned me that the witch I was going to be with was an idiot," the cat said, and I opened my eyes to find her carefully licking one of her front paws. I looked up at Kaillie, on whose face a small smile flittered.

"You think I'm insane, don't you?" I said, biting my lip. "I am insane. There's no other explanation for this."

"Actually, there is," Kaillie replied. "I believe you have just found your familiar."

"My familiar?"

"Obviously," the cat replied without so much as looking up at me.

"A familiar is an animal who is closely linked to you. The magical world decides when it is you need a familiar. A witch can talk to her familiar, and the familiar can talk to her as well. So if you're hearing the cat talk, that means the magical world has decided it's time for you to have one. It makes sense, really. Familiars often come into a witch's life at a time of change. That definitely applies to you right now."

I stared at the cat. "So I can talk to you?" I asked it, and it carefully licked a paw.

"Of course. Goodness, no one warned me I was getting a stupid witch."

"I'm not stupid, I'm just new to this whole magic thing," I shot back. Great, I was talking to pets now.

"Whatever you say. Anyway, I suppose I should give you some credit for getting me out of the water. Although, for the record, I was completely fine, and I totally could have swum back to shore on my own."

I bit back a smile. "Yes, I'm sure you could have. It definitely seemed that way. Why were you in the water, anyway?"

"I was told to wait for you on the beach, and that you would show up there so I could introduce myself to you. Then, I spotted a couple of fish in the water. They looked delicious, and I'm not one to pass up a free meal, so I decided to hunt them. I got a little bit further out to sea than I had expected, and I was just going to turn around and make my way back to shore when you swam out to get me."

"Ah," I replied. "So it was a hunting excursion gone wrong."

"Not wrong, no. Just a little bit longer than I expected."

"Well, did you get the fish?"

"Maybe they got away. But it was close!"

"Then if you didn't get the fish your excursion went wrong. What's your name, anyway?"

"Cleopawtra," the cat replied. "But I suppose you can call me Cleo."

"Cleo," I repeated. "That's a nice name."

"A queen such as myself deserves the best of names."

"Yup, I'm definitely getting the impression that you're a queen," I said. "Now, I don't think you're allowed in the main part of the coffee shop, can you stay here for a few hours until we close without getting your fur into any of the food?"

Cleo sniffed like I had insulted her. "Excuse me, I am a majestic creature, far superior to you witches, wizards and humans in every way. If anybody should be banned from somewhere it's you. But since you've asked so nicely, I suppose I can find a warm space to sleep for a few hours."

"Thanks," I said to Cleo as she wandered over toward the now-off oven. She hopped on top of it with a single graceful leap.

"Mmm, residual heat, this is perfect," she said as she curled herself up into a little ball.

"Great. I'll be back in a few hours," I said to Cleo as I headed back toward the door.

"Thanks for the help, Kaillie. Cleo is on top of that oven, just so you know."

"Perfect, thanks for the heads up. Oh, you'll need one more thing before you go back out there." Kaillie grabbed her wand off the counter again and pointed it at my feet. *"Oh god Saturn, you make people free, now I need some shoes for Eliza's feet."*

A brand-new pair of sneakers appeared out of nowhere on my feet and I let out a laugh. "You know, it's still weird to have magic like this just happen."

"It must be," Kaillie said with a kind nod. "But you'll get used to it. I promise."

"Thanks again for the help," I said with a wave as I made my way back out to where Leanne was busy serving a couple of customers.

I couldn't believe it. I had a pet. I'd never had a pet before. Or, well, a familiar.

I was so glad I'd rescued Cleo from the ocean.

CHAPTER 24

"Hi, Irene," I said with a smile to the woman who was next in line as Leanne went to make the previous customer's coffee. I was really starting to get to know a few of the regulars here at the coffee shop. Irene was the owner of the one dairy farm in town. She ran it on her own, and made her own cheeses there. Kaillie had told me a few days earlier the macaroni and cheese at the small café on her farm was the best she had ever tasted, and I made a mental note to stop by as soon as I got a chance.

"Hello, Eliza," Irene said to me with a warm smile. "Busy killing off some more customers today?"

"You know it," I replied with a wry smile. I'd quickly learned that Irene had a very unique sense of humor.

"Well, I'll take a large coffee and muffin, light on cyanide."

"Coming right up," I said. "Wait, did you say no cyanide, or extra cyanide?"

Irene laughed, a throaty, genuine laugh. "I do like you. Not enough people are willing to laugh about their own impending arrest for murder. Anyway, light on the cyanide. Although, if my daughter comes back from school with another note from her teacher about bad behavior I might have to change my answer."

I laughed as I got the coffee cup and filled it for Irene. Honestly, I wasn't entirely comfortable laughing about how everyone thought I was a murderer, but I also didn't want to seem like a stick-in-the-mud, either.

Irene winked at me as she was about to leave. "Don't worry about Ron. He's terrible at his job, and everyone knows it. You're not going to be arrested, and if you are, I know of at least a few people who would happily storm the prison to let you out."

I laughed awkwardly as Irene left, then turned to Leanne. "Is she always so…"

"Weird?" Leanne finished. "Yeah. That's Irene. I think being around all those cows for her whole life has messed up her sense of humor a little. But the cheese she makes is absolutely primo. And for what it's worth, she's right about some things – for example, we *would* go out of our way to break you out of jail if you got arrested."

"Thanks," I said with a laugh.

"What was with you coming in soaking wet earlier? And what was in your arms?"

I explained the whole situation to Leanne, who at the end of it was practically melting on the floor.

"Oh my goodness! You have a kitty! And you saved her from drowning! Ahh, that's the cutest story I've ever heard! I need to go meet her!"

And before I knew what was happening, Leanne had rushed back into the kitchen to meet Cleo, leaving me alone at the counter hoping against all hope that no one would come in for the next minute or so wanting anything that needed the fancy espresso machine.

Luckily, the next customer to walk through the door was Aunt Lucy. She was closely followed by three other women, two of whom I recognized from the other day at Otterly Delicious, and the other one who bore such a strong resemblance to Leanne that I knew she had to be her mom.

"Hi, Aunt Lucy," I said with a smile. "And hello to you other ladies. What can I do for you this morning?"

"We heard about Ronald coming in this morning and giving you a little bit of trouble," Aunt Lucy replied. "Wanted to see if there was anything we could do to help."

"It's darned stupid," Dorothy said with a nod. "I told my Joe he had better make sure that oaf doesn't do anything to ruin that poor girl's life. Can you imagine? A niece of Lucy's accused of murder! All because Ronald Jones is a buffoon who couldn't solve a real crime if his life depended on it."

The other women all nodded.

"We were thinking we might make our way down to the police station and show off a certain photo," Lucy said to me in a hushed whisper. "But I don't have a copy of it."

"Oh, here, I'll Airdrop it to you. Pass me your phone and I'll do it."

"Please, I know how Airdrop works," Aunt Lucy said, tapping away, and I had to give her credit. I had assumed based on her age that she had no idea how to use it, but sure enough, a moment later 'Lucy's iPhone' popped up as a person I could send the photo to. I did so, and she winked at me. "Perfect. Time to go stir up some trouble. Let's go, ladies! We have an idiotic police chief to go take care of."

"Come back and let me know how it goes," I called after Lucy as she and the Floozies left the coffee shop.

"Will do!" my aunt called back with a wave over her shoulder. To be honest, I was kind of bummed that I couldn't go along with them. It sounded like I was about to miss something fairly exciting.

Leanne reappeared a moment later. "Well, I'm going to steal your familiar," she told me. "That is the most beautiful cat I have ever seen. You need to start an Instagram account for her. She could be famous, like Nala, the cat who just launched her own brand of cat food."

I laughed. "I'm not totally sure Cleo would be into that. I figure maybe I should focus on trying to get to know her, first."

"She's adorable, and I love her. She's young, too. Can't be much more than a kitten. I can't believe you saved her from the ocean."

"Yeah, I've never been that cold in my life. Thank goodness for magic. Kaillie was able to take care of that, or I'm not sure either one of us would have made it."

"Well, at least now you know not to go swimming in the ocean in early spring," Leanne grinned. "I wish I had a familiar. Can you really talk to her?"

I nodded. "Yeah. I thought I was going crazy at first, because she was talking to me. I thought maybe I got brain damage from the swim, or something like that. But no, it turned out there really was a cat that was talking to me."

"That's so cool. Man, I wish I had magical powers. I want a familiar."

"Well, we can always go to an animal shelter and find you a cat," I suggested. "After all, if I move in with you guys, maybe Cleo would like a feline companion to hang out with during the day." There I went again, making permanent plans. This time, I felt my heart squeeze at the idea that I might have to leave here. I really did like my new family that I had discovered.

"That's actually a good idea," Leanne mused. "I've always wanted a cat. We never had pets growing up. Dad never had a familiar, probably because he's allergic to anything with fur. I guess the universe realized he wasn't a prime candidate. But now that I've moved out, there's nothing stopping me getting one of my own. I think I'm going to do it. Good idea, thanks!"

"No problem," I laughed.

"You have to make sure Cleo is ok with it first, though," Leanne said solemnly. "I don't want her feeling annoyed about it. And maybe we should wait until you've moved in with us too, let her settle in."

"I'll have a chat with her and let you know what she thinks," I replied. I was moved by how much my cousin cared about the impact her own new pet would have on Cleo, but also by the way Leanne spoke about me moving in with them so matter-of-factly, like it was a completely normal and acceptable thing that she had no problem with.

I really hoped Aunt Lucy's conversation with Chief Jones was going to have a good outcome for me.

I got my answer about thirty minutes later, when Lucy and the Floozies came right back into the coffee shop, with my aunt at the head of the pack like she always was.

"So? How did it go?" I asked.

"Well, it wasn't exactly what I was hoping for," Aunt Lucy said with a grimace. "I showed Chief Ron the letter, and he told me it proved absolutely nothing. He didn't even want a copy of it. I accused him of being an incompetent drunk, and he threatened to arrest me for breaking and entering in Don's shop."

I groaned. "Great. That means he must have known

about the letter. How else would he have known where it came from?"

"Exactly. So he's willfully ignoring actual evidence. So, Dorothy is going to give Joe the picture, and hopefully some of the *real* cops in this town will take care of this investigation."

My heart sunk. "This sucks. I'm never going to be able to clear my name."

"Never say never," Aunt Lucy said. "And don't worry. I have a plan on how I'm going to get back at Ron. He's going to regret the day he ever decided he was going to frame *my* niece for murder. Come on, ladies. We have some more investigating to do!"

For the second time that day, Lucy and the Floozies filed out of the coffee shop, out to create more havoc and trouble. I could only hope that this time, more came out of it.

"Ron is an idiot," Leanne muttered as they left. "I can't believe they still let him have a job here."

"I just wish he thought the killer was *anyone* except me. I wish the whole town thought it was someone else."

"We'll figure it out," Leanne said. "I mean, we have a limited list of suspects. There's no way someone managed to slip Leonard the poison before he came to the coffee shop; it was too quick-acting. So it had to be one of the people who saw him after he came in here. That really limits things, and makes it much easier for us to figure out."

"Yeah, you're right," I said.

"But you never know. Kaillie and I will come over to Aunt Debbie's for dinner again tonight. We'll figure it all out from there, ok? Maybe we should start over, look at everything from the very beginning. You never know what we may have missed."

"Sure," I replied. "That sounds good."

Maybe it was a good idea. After all, starting over from scratch and looking at the whole murder investigation all over again might trigger something in my memories.

After we closed up for the afternoon, I went and got Cleo from her spot on top of the oven. It was still just a little bit warm, and I was kind of jealous that having a nap on it was how she'd spent her last few hours.

"Come on, little cat, time to go home," I told her, and Cleo meowed unhappily at me as I picked her up.

"I was comfortable there!"

"Yeah, well, the residual heat would eventually go away and I'm heading home, so unless you want to spend the night here, I suggest you come along."

"Fine, fine," Cleo muttered, her eyes looking around the room carefully. She really was absolutely stunning. Naturally, I thought all cats were adorable, and Cleo was no exception. But she was also a truly beautiful cat. Cleopawtra was the perfect name for her; she definitely reminded me of the Egyptian queen.

I said goodbye to Kaillie and Leanne, telling them I would see them at dinner.

"Do you need a ride back?" Debbie asked, and I shook my head.

"No, thanks. I'm just going to walk around a bit, I think. Try and think things over."

"Alright," Aunt Debbie said. "Don't listen to what people around town are saying, ok? The killer is going to be found. Your name will be cleared."

"Yeah," I muttered. "I hope so." I only wished I shared my aunt's confidence.

CHAPTER 25

With that I left the coffee shop, and Cleo and I began walking down the street.

I hated that I wasn't sure if the stares I was getting were from people who thought I was a murderer, or from people who though it was crazy to walk a cat down Main Street.

"Wow, she's so well trained," one woman commented. "You don't even need a leash for her."

"Please, I would never stoop so low as to wear a *leash*," Cleo said haughtily. I had to pretend not to hear her; I didn't want to be not only the woman who had murdered Leonard Steele but *also* the crazy woman who thought her cat spoke to her.

Eventually we reached the end of Main Street.

"I figure you've had enough of the beach for one day? I know I have," I said to Cleo, who agreed.

"Yeah. I still can't believe those stupid fish got away from me."

"Alright. Well, let's head back home. It's about a twenty minute walk. Then I'll have to figure out what to get you for dinner."

"I'm a big fan of fresh salmon."

"I bet you are, but that doesn't mean you're going to get to eat it every day," I said with a smile.

As I walked back toward Aunt Debbie's house, I couldn't help but think about what Leanne had said. We should start thinking about the case all over, in case we missed something. But, what if we had gotten the entire assumption wrong in the first place?

After all, the best suspect was Roman. He had all the reason in the world to murder his brother, and didn't seem the least bit upset that he was dead. But on the other hand, he hadn't been in the coffee shop. So how could he have poisoned Leonard if he hadn't had access to the coffee?

And then it hit me.

The poison had been in Leonard's system. But no one had said it was in the coffee cup.

"Hey Cleo, I think I solved the murder," I said to my new familiar.

"Oh, a murder, that sounds cool. Who died?"

"A local guy. Hold on. I don't know what to do."

"Well, go and tell the cops, and they'll arrest him."

"That's a problem; I don't have any actual evidence," I replied. I had a theory, but that was all it was.

"How do you go and get some evidence?"

I bit my lip. "I don't know. I could go and see him. See if I accuse him, if he would admit to it. I could record it, and then the police chief would have no choice but to arrest him."

"Perfect," Cleo said. "I can use my claws to threaten him." She showed off her paw-knives and I laughed.

"Well, hopefully it won't come to that."

I pulled out my phone and texted Leanne. I needed to know where Roman lived. I was tempted to tell her what I was going to do. After all, she'd probably want to come along. But my fingers paused over the keys before typing it.

I was so used to doing everything on my own that it just felt more right. More natural. Even bringing Cleo along on this trip felt a bit strange. But at least she was a cat; it was a little bit different to a person.

Leanne texted me an address and directions a moment later.

Why, what's up? she texted back a moment later. I stared at the phone again, wondering if I should let her into the loop. But I eventually decided against it. I had gone my whole life without help from anyone except Dad. He was gone now, so I was going to do this myself.

I sent back a thank you text, without answering the second part, and opened up the maps app. Roman lived on the far end of the island, it looked like it was about a fifteen minute walk toward the sea.

"Ok, Cleo. We're going to take a bit of a detour." As we got closer and closer, I started to feel a bit more apprehensive about the whole idea. Once we got off Main Street and started walking down the smaller roads, everything seemed a lot more isolated, and I began to wonder if maybe I should have told Leanne where I was going after all.

No, I wasn't going to do that. I was going to prove that I could do things without others. I had lived my whole life that way, and I wasn't about to change now just because I had found a new group of people that I was genetically related to. It had always been me and Dad, and now it was just me. I could do this on my own.

Steeling myself, I spotted a half-rotted mailbox on the side of the road perched precariously on top of a pole with the house number on it. Well, most of the house number, anyway. One of the '5's had disappeared, but I was fairly certain that was the right place.

"This is how horror movies start, isn't it?" I asked Cleo as we walked down the lane. I was surrounded by fir trees that rose so high into the sky they hid all the light from the sun; it felt closer to seven o'clock than just after three.

"I don't know, I've never seen a horror movie," Cleo replied. "However, a queen never gives up in the face of battle."

"That's a good point," I muttered as we continued along. After walking probably a hundred yards on from the mailbox I spotted the shack which Roman and Leonard must have shared, and it was just as tattered and worn as I had been led to believe. Honestly, it was a miracle the place was still standing. The timber boards that made up the walls were old and leaning precariously to the right. The tin roof seemed to have shifted over the years and there was a gaping hole in one side; it had to be hellish whenever there was a storm.

The yard was littered with rusty bits of old equipment. There was a small tractor missing its wheels that had been tipped onto its side, and a wheelbarrow with a flat tire that looked like it hadn't been moved since the Civil War.

"This looks like the kind of place where mean Rottweilers chase cats around," Cleo muttered next to me.

"I agree. Feel free to run if you see a dog coming after you."

"I'm very good at taunting them from up in the trees."

"Good," I said with a small laugh. I had to admit though, I was nervous. This idea seemed worse with every passing minute. But I was here now, so what did I have to lose?

I pulled out my phone and set up the voice recording app. Now, if Roman came out and I could get him to admit what he'd done, I'd have proof.

Of course, if he killed me and hid my body no one would ever know either.

I pushed that thought aside and slipped the phone back into my pocket.

"Roman?" I called out. This seemed like the kind of place that would be booby-trapped, and I didn't want to find myself suddenly hanging in a net fifteen feet above the ground. "Roman, it's Eliza, the woman from the coffee shop. The new one."

"Go away! Private property!" came Roman's voice a minute later from inside the house.

"Roman, can I talk to you?" I asked. "It's about your brother."

The man came out from the front door then, and I gasped as I took a step backwards. He was holding a shotgun, and he had it aimed right at me.

"I told you, private property."

"Look," I said, holding up my hands. "I don't want any trouble. I was just hoping we could talk."

My mouth went dry as I looked at the gun. The more time passed, the more I thought this was a stupid idea. I had badly overstepped, and I should just leave.

"What do you want to talk about?" Roman snarled.

"Nothing. Never mind, you're right. I'll just go," I said, taking a careful step backwards.

Roman put the gun down. "It's the shotgun, isn't it?"

"It's just a little intimidating."

"Fine," he said, putting it down on the stoop and

taking a couple steps toward me. "What did you want to talk about?"

Part of me wanted to run away as fast as I could back toward town. But if I did that, I might never get my answer. So I took a deep breath as I collected myself.

CHAPTER 26

"You're the one who killed Leonard, aren't you?" I asked when Roman had taken enough steps away from his gun for me to be comfortable accusing him. If he tried to get it I was fairly certain I could run back toward the road and be far enough away that he'd miss me by the time he got the gun.

In response, Roman laughed. "Think you've got it all figured out, do you? But I wasn't in the coffee shop when he was poisoned."

"No, you weren't, but you're the one who swapped out the medicine in his new blood pressure medication for the ground wolfsbane. You didn't *have* to be in the coffee shop. All you had to do was swap the pills at home. Maybe you didn't even know he was going to take that pill that day, you just put the poisoned pill back in the bottle and waited for nature to take its course. But that's how you did it. I'm right, aren't I?"

Roman laughed, but there was no humor in the sound. "So you finally figured it out. I knew it wouldn't be that idiot Jones. You won't get me to admit it publicly, though. Everyone here thinks you did it. I have to admit, your arrival in town worked out pretty well."

"So it's true, then. You put the poisoned pill in with all the others?"

"That's right. He always took two pills with him to work. Took one at the beginning of his shift, and one at the coffee shop at the end of it. Regardless, it wouldn't be able to be tracked back to me."

"All because he didn't want to sell your land."

"Yes. He wasn't being practical about it. How do you think we've eked out an existence for the last few decades? It's been ridiculous. Look at this house! We've been poor our entire lives, and here was a chance for us to finally live like we deserved. We were both old. I'm old. I don't want to have to keep doing upkeep to this stupid shack until I'm eighty. I want to live out my years in the luxury afforded to me by this deal."

"Right, and so to do that you decided your brother shouldn't get to live out his years at all."

Roman shrugged. "He didn't deserve to have nice things. He's the one who insisted on our mother being cremated, going directly against her wishes. So I just went against his wishes to keep breathing."

I shook my head, incredulous at how calmly Roman simply admitted to murdering his brother. He didn't seem to have any regrets, or feel guilty in any way. I had totally misjudged him that day in the coffee shop.

On the bright side, because the recording in my pocket should have been working, I would have his entire admission on my phone. Now all I had to do was get out of here.

Cleo had wandered away at some point; I assumed she was still nearby.

"Alright," I said. "Well, now that I know the truth, I'll be going."

"Not so fast," Roman said, pulling a handgun from the back of his jeans. I gasped as he pointed the barrel right at me. "Now that you know the truth, you don't get to leave."

"I won't tell anyone," I lied. "Who's going to believe me, anyway? As you said, I'm the new person in town, and you've been here forever. It's much more likely that I killed Leonard."

Roman laughed again. "Right. Because I trust you not to tell anyone. You're probably recording this conversation secretly."

Whoops.

"I'm not," I lied. My throat was starting to close up; I was scared. I was really, really scared. I didn't want to die. My life might not have been going perfectly lately, but it was still my life. I wanted to see how it would all play out. I didn't want it to end here, being shot by a murderer trying to get away with it.

And yet, I had no idea what to do. I just hoped Cleo got as far away from here as possible. Hopefully she was smart enough to see the gun and leave.

I took a deep breath to try and calm myself down, and held up my hands.

"There's no need for this, Roman. You're not going to get away with two murders."

"Please. There's going to be no need for me to get away with another murder. You're going to have an accident. Your body will wash ashore in a few hours, and people will think that you decided to end it all out of guilt after you killed Leonard. Now come on, there's no time to waste." He motioned with the gun for me to start walking, and I didn't really see what choice I had.

I eyed the weapon carefully as I stepped in the direction Roman wanted me to go. I quickly saw where he was leading me: a thin path led away from the house, toward the water.

"You don't have to do this," I said as we began walking along the path, my eyes constantly glancing toward the gun. "I'm telling you, this is a bad idea. People know I'm here. People won't think I killed myself. They know I'm investigating. It will come back to you. You've only killed one person so far, you don't have to kill two."

I was really just throwing any idea I could come up with at the wall and hoping one of them stuck.

"Yeah, yeah. Shut your mouth. Nothing's going to save you anymore. There's nothing you can do to stop me, and nothing you can do to save yourself. You're going to go into the water, and that's where you're going to die."

I was well aware of just how right Roman was about the dying thing. Just a few hours ago I had gone into the water for probably about two, maybe three minutes, and I had barely managed to make it back to shore with Cleo. And even then, I probably would have been in trouble if it wasn't for Kaillie's magic immediately warming me back up.

Magic! I was a witch. I had magical powers. In fact, I had a wand in the pocket of my jacket right now. The problem was I had no idea how to cast a spell that might be useful. I could change the color of the gun from black to green, sure. But that wasn't exactly going to be helpful.

Still, I gripped the wand, almost more for emotional support than anything. Roman was walking about ten feet behind me, careful to make sure I wouldn't be able to attack him before he could get a shot off. I needed an advantage, but I just didn't know how to get one.

The sound of the ocean roared in my ears now; I could see the edge of the small cliff I was going to be thrown from to my death. I probably had less than two minutes to come up with a plan before I would be unceremoniously shoved to my demise.

I vowed not to make it easy for him. I wouldn't just

throw myself into the sea. Either Roman would have to shoot me – and when my body came to shore they would know I had been murdered – or he would have to shove me in himself, in which case I would do my best to take him with me.

I might have been about to die, but in the words of Dylan Thomas I was not about to go gentle into that good night. I steeled myself, ready for the fight ahead.

Just then, a rustling came from the bushes nearby. I turned to see what had happened when a black blur suddenly darted out of the trees and jumped toward Roman. There was a glimmer of white teeth, then a howl of pain as Cleo bit down on his arm, hard.

"What the? Get off! Get off me, you crazy animal!"

Roman shook his arm, trying to get my cat to let it go, and the gun exploded. Pain ripped through the upper part of my arm and I let out a yelp, clasping my hand to it. Still, this was my chance. I ran back toward Roman and collided with him. We both went flying, the gun fell to the ground, and Cleo darted back off into the woods.

"Run, Cleo!" I called out to her. "Get away from him!"

I scrambled to my feet as quickly as my injured arm would allow me to and began running back along the path toward the house. There was no time to try and find the gun. My best chance of escape was to take advantage of these precious few seconds.

I looked around and spotted Cleo in front of me. "Go," I called to her. "You have to escape."

"Not without you," she panted back.

"You've already saved me once," I said.

"That makes us even."

I was touched by my cat's insistence on staying with me. As I rushed through the forest I didn't bother checking behind me. I didn't want to waste precious seconds to see if Roman was catching up to me, which was why, when I finally reached the house, I was shocked to see him standing there, the gun leveled right at me.

"What?" I said, blood leaving my face, and he grinned.

"You forget I've lived on this property my entire life. I know every single inch of it like the back of my hand. Now, I'm going to kill you, and then I'm going to kill that meddlesome cat of yours, too."

I looked down to see that Cleo had disappeared once more. Thank goodness. More than anything I wanted her to get away.

Roman stepped toward me, the gun leveled at my chest. I couldn't breathe. I couldn't speak. All I could do was stare at that barrel, knowing that I was about to die.

"Right, you're too much trouble to get rid of the way I'd planned," he said. "I'm just going to shoot you and leave your body in the woods. You won't be found for years, I promise you that. Any last words?"

I couldn't even shake my head. All I thought about was Dad. Dad, who had made me promise when he was on his deathbed that I was going to live my life the best way I knew how. Dad, who had always been there for me, and assured me that no matter what I did in life, he was proud of me. Dad, who told me in those precious few minutes we had as his heart was failing that his greatest regret was that he was never going to walk me down the aisle.

Well, Dad, you didn't miss out on that. I was never going to get to walk down that aisle. As it turned out, we were going to be reunited a lot sooner than I had expected.

I wanted to close my eyes. I didn't want to see what was coming. But I couldn't do it. It was like every muscle in my body was frozen in place.

Suddenly, I saw movement behind Roman, and he crumpled to the ground without a sound. The gun fell harmlessly to the side, and I gaped at my savior. It was Leanne.

She was holding a shovel, staring down at the unmoving Roman like she couldn't believe what she'd just done.

"Leanne," I said quietly. "You... you saved me."

"I did, didn't I?" she replied, dropping the shovel. I ran over to the gun and grabbed it, then checked Roman for a pulse. It was weak, but it was there.

"We have to call for help," I said. Leanne nodded and pulled out her phone. I stared down at Roman while I heard Leanne speaking in the background, and Cleo made her way toward me, wrapping herself around my legs.

"Did you go and get Leanne?" I asked.

"No," Cleo replied. "I was running up the road like you told me to and I saw her. As soon as I did, I led her straight here."

"Thank you," I said. "You've saved my life twice today."

"Well, you know, I am a queen among cats. A heroic action or two isn't completely out of the ordinary for me. Although I would enjoy payment in the form of fresh salmon."

"Done," I replied. "I promise I'll get you some, although it might be a while before we're allowed to leave here."

Leanne hung up the phone. "The police will be here in a few minutes. It looks like it's all over."

I had never been more relieved in my life.

CHAPTER 27

Five minutes later Detective Ross Andrews showed up, followed closely by a couple of EMTs carrying a stretcher. They immediately began taking care of Roman while Detective Andrews carefully led me off to the side.

"Are you alright?" he asked me at first, and I nodded.

"Yeah. I mean, I think so. Maybe ask me again in a day or two when I've had time to process what just happened."

"Good instincts," Detective Andrews said. "You're running on adrenaline right now, I'm sure. But I do need you to tell me what happened while it's fresh in your mind." Then, he noticed the bleeding of my arm.

"Were you shot?"

I looked over at the cut. It stung like crazy, but I had to admit, it didn't look that bad. It appeared the bullet had just grazed my arm, and a small incision in the side of my arm bled.

"Oh. Yeah, I was."

Detective Andrews immediately called over one of the paramedics, who instantly began to take care of the wound, wrapping it in gauze and giving me care instructions.

"Are you sure you're alright?" Detective Andrews asked, and I nodded.

"Yeah. Thanks."

He flipped open to a new page in his notebook while I recounted the entire story. I pulled my phone from my pocket, turned off the recording, and handed it to him. "If you don't believe me, it should all be there, anyway. I recorded the whole thing."

"Well, there's nothing Chief Jones will be able to say about that," Detective Andrews replied with a grim smile. "Thank you for this. Although, I do need to ask what it was that convinced you coming here by yourself to confront a murderer was a good idea."

I sighed. "No one believed me. Everyone in town thought I was a killer. I couldn't live here with that hanging over my head, so when I realized it was Roman, I thought I could get him to admit it to me, and then I'd be able to leave. I never thought he'd try to kill me, too."

"Yes, it was lucky that your cat here managed to attack him," Detective Andrews said, reaching down and scratching Cleo under the chin. She mewed in appreciation; she was obviously already a fan of the detective.

"It was," I said. "And that Leanne came, as well."

"Yes, why was she here?" Detective Andrews asked, and I shrugged.

"I'm not sure. You'll have to ask her. But oh boy, am I ever glad she came."

"So am I," Detective Andrews replied, his eyes softening. "You're very lucky to be alive, but I'm glad you are. You should have come to me. I'm trained to deal with murderers."

"Would you have believed me, though?" I asked.

"Yes," he replied firmly. "Unlike most people in town, I don't jump straight to conclusions. I know there are bad people everywhere. I go where the evidence takes me. Of course, you were ahead of me there. I didn't realize the poison was in the pill, and not in the coffee. It was a stupid mistake that I should have caught."

"Did you test the coffee?"

"We sent it out for testing, but the results aren't back yet. Chief Jones only put a rush on the toxicology report for Leonard's body. I'm sure in a day or two when we get that report back it'll show there was no poison in the coffee itself."

"Yeah," I said with a nod.

"I'm serious, though. I'm glad you're alright, but I wish you'd come to me. If you ever have any more issues with people in town, please do come and see me."

"Ok, thanks," I said.

"Now, I'm sure I'll need to speak with you a few more times in the coming days, but for now I think you'd probably like to be getting home."

"I would," I replied. Detective Andrews spoke with Leanne for a few minutes, and I sat on the stoop with Cleo, absent-mindedly stroking her fur while I waited, until finally Leanne made her way back to me and held out a hand to help me up.

"Want to head home?"

"Absolutely."

"Good. Aunt Debbie made beef stew for dinner."

"That sounds like exactly the sort of meal I need right now."

"Only if it's topped with salmon," Cleo chimed in. The three of us began walking up the lane back toward the road.

"Thanks for saving my life," I said to Leanne.

"Hey, what is family for?"

"How did you know to come?"

"When you didn't tell me what you were doing, I got worried. Then, I called Aunt Debbie and asked if you came home, and she said no. I thought maybe you were in trouble, so I came to investigate."

"But..." I started. "You barely even know me."

Leanne laughed. "Don't be silly. I might not know

you, but you're family. Of course I'm going to do everything I can to help you. That's what family does."

Maybe it was just the emotion of the day, but tears welled up in my eyes. I tried to blink them away, but they fell to my cheeks instead. I couldn't believe Leanne had come to my rescue just because we were genetically related.

It had always been just me and Dad. I had never known a bigger family than that. And yet, I knew Dad would have done the same thing. He would have had my back, the same way that Leanne did.

"Are you alright?" Leanne asked, realizing I was crying, and I nodded.

"Yeah. I'm just a bit overwhelmed. You're amazing. All of you are amazing."

Leanne wrapped her arm around my shoulders. "Just because we didn't know you for the last twenty-something years doesn't mean you're not family. You're one of us now. I want you to know that."

I smiled through my tears and leaned my head against Leanne's shoulder as we walked toward her Toyota parked along the road.

I had been so used to doing things alone, and just with Dad my entire life. And yet, as Leanne had just shown me by saving my life, maybe it was time for me to spread my wings a little bit and accept my new family. My magical family.

It was time for me to open up my heart a little bit more.

We drove straight to Aunt Debbie's house, where Kaillie practically sprinted to the car when she saw us.

"Are you guys ok? We heard the police were called to Roman Steele's property. Is that blood on your arm?"

"Yeah, it is. Roman Steele shot Eliza."

"I'm ok though, it was just a flesh wound," I said. "And a real flesh wound, not like the knight from *Monty Python and the Holy Grail*."

Kaillie laughed. "I love that movie. You're sure you're alright, though?"

Before I had a chance to reply in the affirmative, Aunt Lucy came over. "Someone got shot and I wasn't there to see it? What happened? Did anyone die?"

"No one died, Aunt Lucy," Leanne said. "Roman Steele is getting arrested for killing his brother and trying to kill Eliza, though."

"Well, luckily for all of us, Deb has just put dinner on the table, so we can annoy her by talking about murder over stew."

My stomach began to rumble and I realized that since the only thing I'd eaten all day was three quarters of a slice of cake, I was absolutely ravenous. I supposed being hunted down by a raving madman would do that to a person.

"Stew and murder talk sounds great," I said with a laugh, letting the others walk me back into the house.

Aunt Debbie's eyes immediately flew to the gauze wrapped around my arm when I walked into the kitchen. "There's bound to be some magic we can do to fix that," she said, but I shook my head.

"It's fine, thanks. Although, it does sting a bit, so if you have something for pain I'd happily take that."

"Of course I do, dear," Aunt Debbie said, rushing to a closet and pulling out another magical first-aid kit. She grabbed a vial filled with a bright orange fluid that looked remarkably like orange juice, and placed it carefully in my hands, wrapping my fingers around it. "Take one tablespoon every six hours. It will get rid of your pain immediately. And if you're still having problems, come to me and I can make you something stronger."

"You never offered *me* anything stronger when I was in pain," Leanne complained, and Aunt Debbie shot her a look.

"Thankfully, *you've* never been shot before."

"Yeah, well, that doesn't mean I don't deserve the magical morphine," Leanne retorted.

"It does too," Kaillie said, her hands on her hips. "That would be considered misuse of magical potions."

"I've also been shot," Aunt Lucy declared, and the look Aunt Debbie gave her was scathing.

"Lucy, stop setting a bad example for the girls. You can make your own potions if you want them."

"Oh yeah, I can," Aunt Lucy replied with a grin, brightening significantly. "I forgot about that."

I laughed as I made my way to the table, a giant crock-pot full of stew flying inches away from my face and landing with a screech that moved the tablecloth a couple of inches just in front of my plate.

The aroma of beef, vegetables and thyme rose to my nostrils and I immediately began salivating, staring at the stew like it was the first time I was going to eat in weeks.

"You get to serve yourself first," Leanne said to me, motioning for me to have at it. "When you solve a murder and help get a killer off the streets, you get first dibs on dinner."

"Is that the rule now, is it?" Aunt Debbie said with a smile as she handed me the ladle. I didn't need any more encouragement than that and began to scoop out the stew as Aunt Debbie put a hand softly on my shoulder. "I'm very glad you're ok, Eliza."

"Thanks," I told her. "Me too."

As the others all settled themselves around the table for dinner, I looked around. Every single one of these people had accepted me into their homes and into their lives, and I couldn't be more grateful. It had just been me and Dad for all of those years, but now that Dad was gone, I had found family I didn't even know existed.

I couldn't wait to see what the future was going to bring.

Book 2: Whole Latte Magic: Eliza is settling nicely into her new life on Enchanted Enclave. That is, until she and Leanne come across a woman who's been stabbed. Attempted murders have a way of shaking things up a bit.

Leanne feels guilty about how they came across the victim, however, and Eliza isn't about to let her go around solving a stabbing on her own. With Kaillie joining in, the cousins start their own investigation, but it turns out there's more to the victim's life than they initially thought.

With the help of some new friends from Western Woods, Eliza and her cousins quickly hone in on a few suspects. But the stakes are higher than they realize when an attempt is made on their lives as well. Will they be able to solve the case before the attempted murderer is finally successful?

Click or tap here to read Whole Latte Magic now.

ALSO BY SAMANTHA SILVER

Thank you so much for reading! Here's how to keep up with my books in this series and others:

- Sign up for my newsletter to be the first to find out about new releases, and get a free bonus novella from the Western Woods series: http://www.samanthasilverwrites.com/newsletter

- You can also check out the next book in this series, Whole Latte Magic, by clicking here: http://www.samanthasilverwrites.com/wholelattemagic

You can check out my other books, as well. I highly recommend the Pacific North Witches series, which is set in the same world as Enchanted Enclave, but on the paranormal world side:

Going Through the Potions (Book 1)

Get with the Potion (Book 2)

Potion Sickness (Book 3)

Any Potion in a Storm (Book 4)

Or you can discover any of the other series I write by clicking the links below:

Western Woods Mysteries

Pacific Cove Mysteries

Willow Bay Witches Mysteries

Magical Bookshop Mysteries

California Witching Mysteries

Cassie Coburn Mysteries

Ruby Bay Mysteries

ABOUT THE AUTHOR

Samantha Silver lives in British Columbia, Canada, along with her husband and a little old doggie named Terra. She loves animals, skiing and of course, writing cozy mysteries.

You can connect with Samantha online here:
Facebook
Email
For the most up-to-date info and lots of goodies like sneak previews, cover reveals and more, join my Facebook Reader Group by clicking here.

Printed in Great Britain
by Amazon